ALSO BY **DAVID KLASS**

GRANDMASTER

DAVID KLASS

GRANDMASTER

FRANCES FOSTER BOOKS

FARRAR ■ STRAUS ■ GIROUX

NEW YORK

Farrar Straus Giroux Books for Young Readers
175 Fifth Avenue, New York 10010

Printed in the United States of America
Designed by Andrew Arnold
First edition, 2014
1   3   5   7   9   10   8   6   4   2

macteenbooks.com

Library of Congress Cataloging-in-Publication Data
Klass, David.
    Grandmaster / David Klass. — First edition.
        pages cm
    Summary: "A father-son chess tournament reveals the dark side of the game."
—Provided by publisher.
    ISBN 978-0-374-32771-2 (hardback)
    ISBN 978-0-374-32777-4 (e-book)
    [1. Chess—Fiction.   2. Fathers and sons—Fiction.   3. New York (N.Y.)—
Fiction.]   I. Title.

PZ7.K67813Gr 2014
[Fic]—dc23

                                                            2013022075

Farrar Straus Giroux Books for Young Readers may be purchased for business or
promotional use. For information on bulk purchases please contact Macmillan
Corporate and Premium Sales Department at (800) 221-7945 x5442 or by email at
specialmarkets@macmillan.com.

To my two favorite patzers, Gabriel and Madeleine, and to my grandmaster of an editor, Frances Foster

"A mind saturated with one idea to the exclusion of all others is necessarily predisposed to mania, and if a man allows himself to regard Chess as the one fact of existence, thereby starving his mind, which, like the body, requires a variety of food, then the texture of the strongest brain must become weakened, and the reason sooner or later be overthrown."

—William Norwood Potter,
The City of London Chess Magazine, 1876

GRANDMASTER

1

Chess club was done for the day, and so was I. I had played three games that afternoon, two of which I'd managed to lose in the first fifteen moves. I tried to remind myself that I had just taken up the game six months ago and was still learning the basics, but there were times when I wanted to heave the nearest chess set out the window and never touch another rook or pawn again.

I pulled on my coat and headed out the door. Suddenly a hand yanked me back into the empty room and I found myself alone with the two senior co-captains of the chess team, Eric Chisolm and Brad Kinney. "We need to talk to you, Patzerface," Eric said as Brad locked the door.

A "patzer" in chess speak is a beginner who barely knows the moves and is a pushover to beat. It's like being called a combination of chump, rookie, and dufus. Given the unfortunate similarity of my name to "patzer," I had been called it many times since I first walked in the door of the chess club. But "Patzer-face" was a new twist by the co-captains that I didn't particularly like. "Actually my name's Pratzer," I stammered, glancing from one to the other to try to figure out what was going on.

Eric Chisolm was senior class president, a turbo-charged student and a superachiever with intense black eyes who had never gotten less than an A in his life. He was a grind—maybe not brilliant but he outworked everyone else. He literally could never sit still—even when Eric played chess he was always fidgeting, getting up for water, and pacing behind his chair, probably doing his calculus homework in his head while figuring out a next move that would destroy his opponent. He was the son of a heart surgeon, and everyone knew he was going to be the valedictorian, go to Harvard, and discover the cure for cancer.

Brad Kinney was less intense but more naturally talented. He was tall and rugged, with a grade point average that glittered as brightly as the huge trophies he won as captain of the swimming team and contributed to our school's trophy case. For fun, and maybe to make us all even a little more jealous, he dated the prettiest girl in the freshman class. He was the best chess player in our club—a master at eighteen who regularly won local and regional tournaments.

At another school the two of them probably wouldn't have been caught dead on the chess club, but Loon Lake Academy had the oldest and strongest chess team in New Jersey—the

Looney Knights—and it was cool to be on it, especially if you were Eric Chisolm or Brad Kinney.

I was not Eric or Brad—I was Daniel Pratzer, apparently also known in certain circles as Patzer-face. I was not tall or brilliant or rich. The admissions office must have accepted me because it was a weak year and my combination of mediocre scholarship and undistinguished extracurriculars was just enough to pass muster.

My grade average hovered above C+, resisting all my attempts to lift it into the B range like an airplane that has reached its operational ceiling and can't gain a few more feet of desperately needed altitude. I could play a bunch of sports reasonably well, but the electrifying soccer run and the diving baseball catch forever eluded me. I had decided to join the chess club on a whim. The school sports teams practiced for more than two hours every day, and since I was still struggling with the homework load I didn't have enough free time or ability for them. Chess met every Tuesday, and I thought the club might be a good way to make some new friends.

"We know what your name is, Patzer-face," Eric said. "That's why we need to talk to you."

"What about my name?" I began to ask.

"Sit down and shut your trap," Brad advised with his usual charm.

I sat at a desk and waited nervously. Was this some kind of freshman chess club initiation? Would they do something awful to me with rooks and bishops, leaving scars that would last for the rest of my life? I had only been at Loon Lake Academy for seven months, and had so far managed to fly under the radar of the cool-and-cruel crowd.

I glanced from one senior co-captain to the other and tried to figure out what these two towering school icons could possibly want from me.

"What are you doing this weekend?" Eric asked.

"Nothing special," I told him. "Staying home. Watching some junk on TV. Rethreading my sheets."

"Rethreading your what?"

"It was a joke," I explained.

"His sense of humor's worse than his chess playing," Eric grunted to Brad.

"You're not going to be rethreading anything this weekend," Brad told me. "Don't make any plans."

"What's this about?"

Brad plunked his big frame down on the desk next to my chair and folded his arms, staring at me with his bright blue eyes. It didn't seem fair that a guy who could swim fifty meters in thirty seconds and had the physique of a Viking raiding-party chieftain was also a chess master, with a rating well above the 2200 norm. "We know about your father," Brad announced.

"Huh?" I gulped. What was there to know about Morris Pratzer except that he was the shortest, baldest, and no doubt poorest father to ever send a child to Loon Lake Academy? He was practically mortgaging our house so that his only son could go to this fancy private school.

I don't mean to be critical—my dad's a good guy who works

long hours at his accounting firm and sacrifices everything for his family. He also has a lighter side and some notable hidden talents that he sometimes reveals at parties: he can wiggle his ears, arch his eyebrows in opposite directions, and do a half-decent Elvis impersonation, but he's not the sort of "A-Lister" that people suddenly dig up revelations about.

"There's a chess tournament this weekend in New York," Eric said, as if that explained everything.

"Didn't see it on our schedule . . ." I replied cautiously. The truth is I rarely looked at the tournament schedule because I wasn't on the five-member travel team. Nor was I on the seven-member backup team. I was on the euphemistically titled Regular Reserve Roster, which meant they would use me when necessary—which was no doubt never unless a comet struck Loon Lake and killed the dozen players ahead of me.

"That's 'cause it's not a regular school tournament," Brad cut me off. "It's a new kind of tournament. A father-son tournament. Each team needs six players to enter—three fathers and three sons. It's at the Palace Royale Hotel in New York City. There's twenty thousand dollars in prize money. Ten grand for first place. Do you understand now?"

No, I didn't understand. Eric and Brad were strong players and I knew their fathers were both experts, but I was a patzer and my dad had never played a game of chess in his life. When I joined the club and brought some pieces home, I offered to teach him how they moved. "No thanks, Daniel," he said, laughing. "I don't have the mind for it."

I looked back at Eric and Brad and shook my head. "I don't get it. I won't help you much and my dad doesn't play."

Eric dug out a piece of paper. I saw that it was some kind of computer printout. "Your father is Morris W. Pratzer?" he asked, like a prosecuting attorney nailing an evasive witness.

"Yeah."

"We needed one more father-son to join us so we ran the dads of all club members through the Chess Federation ratings database, going back three decades."

He showed me the paper. My father's name and rating were there with an asterisk because his rating hadn't changed in almost thirty years. I stared at it. According to the printout, Morris W. Pratzer had been a grandmaster, rated well over 2500. "This is a mistake," I said. "Don't you think I'd know it if my father was a grandmaster?"

"Apparently not, Patzer-face," Eric said.

"Go home and have a father-son chat," Brad urged, handing me a sheet with info about the tournament. "Find out the source of this little misunderstanding. Tell your dad we humbly invite him to join us this weekend in Manhattan, and if Grandmaster Pratzer doesn't show up we'll wring his son's neck."

2

My mom had cooked a meat loaf that night, with broccoli and rice pilaf. She isn't a very good cook, but there are a dozen or so meals that are family favorites that she's made so many times over the years she's perfected them. Meat loaf is high on the list, and we were all digging in.

My sister, Kate, sat across from me, trying to eat as little broccoli as possible and get away from the table fast so that she could gab with her friends on her new cell phone. She went to the same crummy public school I had gone to for years. My parents were planning to send her to a private high school, too, when she finished middle school.

With the prospect of two kids in private school looming, my mom had gone back to work as an assistant teacher in the local elementary school. She worked in a first-grade class, and even though she was home by three p.m. most days, she now wore a perpetually tired and harried look, as if platoons of six-year-olds had been attacking her nonstop for hours, bellowing war cries and firing paper wads at her till she was ready to raise the white flag.

"I don't hear anyone talking so I guess the dinner is okay," she said.

"It's delicious, Ruth," my father told her, carving another slice of meat loaf for himself. He wasn't a big man, and he sat in a chair all day doing people's taxes and figuring out their books, so he probably shouldn't have been eating so much. His paunch was expanding into a sizable potbelly. "Kate, chew with your mouth closed, please."

She rolled her eyes at him, but so slowly that it was hard to tell if they were circling in irritation or just moving around the room in an innocent round-about pattern. "Can I be excused?" she asked.

"After you finish your broccoli."

She picked up a tiny floret, broke it in two, and put half of it in her mouth. "Yum," she said. "Can I be excused now?"

"No," my father told her. "And if you roll your eyes at me again, that new phone is going to disappear for a week."

"Great," she said. "Threaten me. What parenting book have you been reading?"

My father let out a sigh, as if to say "I work hard all day and come home to this." He looked at me. "How's school, Daniel? Tell me something fun."

"We dissected rats in bio lab today."

Kate lowered her fork. "That's it. I'm out of here."

"Not till you finish your broccoli," my father told her. "Daniel, that's not suitable dinner conversation."

"Well, we did," I said.

"Especially when we're eating meat loaf," Kate noted, grinding a piece of broccoli against her plate with her fork, as if attempting to break the limp vegetable up into subatomic particles that would then float away into the ether. "Who knows what goes into meat loaf."

"Ground sirloin," my mother said. "There were no rodent ingredients in the recipe. Could we get off this subject?"

"Try again, Daniel," my father said. "Something fun and interesting must have happened today."

I took a deep breath. "Okay. Something unusual did happen in chess club."

"It's kind of hard to believe that anything fun and exciting could happen in a chess club," Kate muttered.

"Go on, Daniel," my mother encouraged me. "I'm sure we'd all like to hear what happened, including your sister."

"There's going to be a tournament in New York this weekend," I said. "They're only bringing three players from the whole team. They want me to come."

"That's exciting," my mom said. "Do you want to go? Will the school pay for it?"

"It's not a regular school tournament," I told her. I was watching my dad as he chewed his meat loaf. "It's a father-son tournament."

His eyes flicked to me for a moment and then quickly down

at his plate. He swallowed the meat loaf he was chewing and had a long drink of water, then slowly put down his fork.

"I'm afraid I don't understand," my mother said.

"Neither did I," I told her. "And I still don't."

"When are we getting to the fun and interesting part?" Kate wanted to know.

"Your dad doesn't play chess," my mom observed.

Dad looked at her and then back at me.

"That's what I told them," I said. "Why would you want my dad? He can't play at all. But they said they had done a computer search on all the team fathers, and he used to play really well."

"They must have had the wrong Morris Pratzer," my mother said. "It's not a common name, but there are dozens of Pratzers out there."

"They had looked up Morris *W.* Pratzer," I told her, emphasizing the middle initial. "You're Morris William Pratzer, right, Pop?"

"Yes," my father answered softly, putting one hand flat on the table as if preparing to resign a chess game.

"According to their information, Morris W. Pratzer was a grandmaster." I heard a little anger creep into my voice. "But that can't be, because if you were a grandmaster, Dad, your son would know about it and not have to be told by a bunch of chess club bozos. Right? If you were a grandmaster, we would be playing games every night, and you would be teaching me openings and endgame theory and helping me out so I wouldn't be just a patzer."

My father stood up from the table and drew himself up to his full height of five feet four inches. His fist came down on the tabletop so hard that it rattled the silverware. "I'm not playing in any chess tournament in New York next weekend, and neither are you, Daniel. You're going to help me clean the basement. Now, excuse me. I've lost my appetite." He walked quickly away from the table.

My mother and I watched him go, and then looked at each other. She stood up and started after him.

"Well, that *was* kind of interesting," Kate admitted to me. Then she shouted: "Hey, Dad, aren't you going to finish *your* broccoli?"

3

He was standing on the back porch, his hands in his pockets, staring up at the half-moon that floated tiredly above this dinky New Jersey town, and I would have felt sorry for him if I hadn't been so angry.

My mom opened the screen door and propelled me toward him with a gentle push. "Go, talk to him, Daniel. He has some good news."

I wondered what kind of a conversation they had just had. After my dad stormed away from the dinner table, Mom had followed him into their room and shut the door. They had talked, often in loud voices, for the better part of an hour.

Kate had gone straight from dinner to her room and was blabbing away on the phone at ten thousand decibels, so even if I had wanted to eavesdrop on my parents, all I could hear was seventh-grade girl talk: "Do you really think he's hot? No, of course I don't like him. Don't make me barf. I mean, he acts like a total dolt, but that look he gives you—oh my God—but he's such a jerk. Where did you hear *that*? No, I swear I don't and never will. But this is what his friend Allen told Susan that Glen overheard him saying about the time we met up at the ice rink and I spilled hot chocolate on him."

I retreated into my own bedroom and took out my algebra homework and tried to lose myself in solving the sorts of problems that actually have logical answers. But my mind kept circling back like a boomerang toward a more difficult and personal mind twister: What kind of father is a master—no, a *grand*master—at something and never tells his family? What possible solution could there be for that? I forced myself to focus on the homework and whipped off a few problems in record time. Math is my best subject. I'm not a genius at it, but I must have inherited some of my dad's numerical ability along with the lousy sports genes.

My father can add twenty four-digit numbers in his head faster than I can punch them into a calculator. "It's no big deal," he always says with a shrug, after amazing people with his party trick. "People are afraid of numbers but numbers are our pals. You just have to let them come in and play around like old friends."

"How can numbers be friends?" I remember thinking at age seven or eight when I first heard him say it, trying to imagine a playdate between numbers 4 and 11, or a water balloon fight between 7 and 52. But when I hit fourth grade, I started seeing patterns that other kids couldn't see, and when I looked at homework or test problems I often leapfrogged to the right answer.

It was as if the numbers were calling out to me: "Hey, Daniel, this is your friend 123. Just plug me in right after the equal sign, old bud. Good to see you again. And give my regards to your dad."

I glanced away from my homework to the trophies on the shelf above my desk. There were more than twenty of them, and not all were merely for participating. I had worked hard to become a decent baseball player, a moderately competitive tennis player, and an acceptable soccer player with a good right foot. But I had never been great at any of them. I was never the go-to guy, the star picked first, the hitter with the Babe Ruth swing who came steaming around third with the coach windmilling his arm and everybody on their feet cheering wildly for a tape-measure home run.

Part of the problem was that I just didn't have the genes for it—my father was unathletic from his nose to his toes. I had inherited his small frame, with a noticeable improvement over the previous generation in strength and coordination. Not only couldn't Dad throw a football in a spiral, but he couldn't toss a baseball overhand more than twenty feet.

Since he had no sports skills himself, I couldn't blame him for never coaching me. What sucked was that he had no interest in my games. I had gone through Little League scanning the bleachers, wondering if he would show up and how long he would stay. I'll never forget coming to bat with the bases loaded in a playoff game, glancing toward the stands, and seeing my dad reading the Sunday *Times*.

I blinked away the vivid memory and tried to concentrate on a multivariable problem. A grocery makes a ten-pound sack of trail mix. They use cashews, raisins, and sunflower seeds. Raisins cost one dollar a pound, sunflower seeds two dollars, and cashews three dollars. The total cost of the sack is sixteen dollars. How much of each ingredient did the store use? I jabbed the pencil into the paper so hard the point snapped off, then laid it down on my desk and just sat there.

A grandmaster. He had actually been a grandmaster. And I had sat up one night in the living room with a plastic chess set, teaching myself the most basic opening theory, and he had been *right there*, watching TV, and said absolutely nothing. A month later I had entered my first tournament and lost all five games and come home with my head hanging. "Maybe you should try something else," he'd suggested. "Any interest in learning to play the trombone?"

It pissed me off that he had hidden this big secret from me, but at the same time I couldn't stop feeling excited and a little proud. Patzer-face's father had really and truly been a grandmaster! How about that?

I had picked up my pencil and was looking for the sharpener when my mom knocked on the door. "Daniel?"

"I'm doing homework."

"Can I come in?"

"Not right now, Mom."

She opened the door. "Sorry, but I think you should come talk to your father."

"About what?"

She walked over to me and kissed the top of my head. "Don't be like that."

"Like what?"

She lowered her voice. "He loves you very much."

"He lied to us."

"He didn't lie. He concealed."

"Cashews and raisins."

She looked at me. "What?"

"I mean, big difference."

"There is a difference. He's a good man, Daniel."

"You married him."

"What's that supposed to mean?"

I could hear the hurt in her voice, so I met her eyes and said, "Look, I know he's a good man, and I love him, too, but he concealed something incredible that I would have liked to have known."

"We all conceal things," she pointed out gently, "and sometimes we have our reasons."

I wondered what he had told her in the bedroom that had gotten her onto his side. My voice rose a little louder. "He told me he didn't know how to play chess. That's not just a lie, Mom. That's a whopper. Let me be mad for a while, and then I'll be okay. Okay?"

"Not okay. Come now."

"Why?"

"Because he's waiting for you. Please, sweetie."

She took my hand and I couldn't fight her. I got up from my desk and let her lead me through the house to the screen door. She opened it and pushed me out.

He must have heard the door close and me step onto the creaky floorboards, but he didn't turn or say anything.

I took a few steps toward him and waited. "Pop?" I finally said. "Or should I call you Grandmaster?"

He turned then, with a sad look on his face. "The boys on your team were right," he admitted in a low voice. "That was me."

"I know they were right," I told him. "What I don't know is why you didn't tell me."

"But on another level, they weren't right," he mused, ignoring my question. "That wasn't me. It was a completely different person, very long ago."

"You have an asterisk next to your name because your rating hasn't changed in a million years, but you're still Morris W. Pratzer," I told him. "Grandmaster titles never go away."

He took his hands out of his pants pockets and let them hang awkwardly at his sides. "I've forgotten it all," he said. "I haven't pushed a pawn in twenty-nine years."

Twenty-nine years? He was not that old a guy. "How young were you when you made grandmaster?"

He hesitated so long that I didn't think he was going to answer. "Sixteen and two months."

"Isn't that some kind of record?"

"Bobby Fischer made grandmaster at fifteen and a half. And since then a couple of players have made it even younger."

"Holy crap," I said. "Fischer did it at fifteen and change, and you were sixteen and two months. You were really a slow-poke."

He read something in my face and shook his head. "Daniel, in your imagination you see some kind of brilliant and glorious chess champion," he said. "But in my memory I see a sad little kid with glasses sitting at a tournament concentrating so hard his stomach feels tied up in double knots."

"That's why you gave it up?" I asked. "Indigestion?"

He shrugged and peered off the back porch into the shadowy darkness of the lawn, as if searching for something lurking out there. "One day in my junior year of high school I had won a tournament," he told me in a near whisper, "and I was coming home in the evening carrying a big trophy. All of a sudden I met two kids from my high school. It was a girl I liked, with a guy I despised. They were coming from a party, arm in arm. I showed them my trophy and she admired it while he sneered at me. Then he led her away, and I watched them walking down the street, laughing together. I walked home alone with my trophy and put it on the shelf and stared at it for a couple of hours. And I never played again."

"Because chess wasn't a good way to get girls?" I asked. "Did quitting help?"

"Chess was not a good way of meeting girls, but it wasn't just that," he told me. "The teenage years are a search for identity. I didn't want to be that boy. I was reaching a serious level of competition. I didn't want to study chess theory for three hours a day. I hated who I was becoming and I guess I just wanted to have more fun."

"So you became an accountant." I regretted it as soon as I had said it.

"Well, MGM didn't call and offer to make me the next James Bond," he noted softly.

"Sorry, Dad."

"I don't hate what I do, Daniel. But I'm very sorry I lied to you about chess. It was painful when I played and painful when I gave it up, but you're my son and I owe you the truth. Let's try to be completely honest with each other going forward."

We stood silently on the porch for several seconds, listening to the crickets fiddling away in the backyard.

"You can make it up to me," I said. "Play this weekend." I hesitated and then added in a very low voice: "They don't respect me at the school. They call me Patzer-face. I want to bring you. It would make me proud."

"Your mother thinks I should play, too." He nodded. "She says we don't spend enough time together, and soon you'll be grown and out the door."

"Don't do it because she wants you to," I told him.

He surprised me by walking over and putting his arm on my shoulder. He's not a demonstrative man, and I couldn't remember the last time he had reached out to me. I pulled back a step, but his hand stayed awkwardly but resolutely atop my shoulder blade. "You really want this?"

"I think it would be fun."

"That's a 'yes'?"

"Don't do it for me either."

He let out a long, tortured sigh. "Okay," he said. "I won't do it for your mother and I won't do it for you and I certainly won't do it for me, because we're operating on a policy of total honesty here, and I don't want to ever play chess again. But yes, I'll do it."

"For who?" I asked, confused.

"*I said I'll do it.* Don't push any more. Just take it or leave it, Daniel."

"I'll take it."

His hand stayed on my shoulder a second more, and then he pulled it back. "With two conditions. First, don't expect too much."

"Come on. It's like riding a bicycle."

"A very rusty old bicycle," he said. "The wheels probably don't even turn."

"We'll oil them. What's the second condition?"

"After this is over, it's over. One tournament. One time. I'll spring for a New York hotel room. We'll have to economize on meals and don't expect Broadway shows. I'll do my best and play my hardest. But that's it. Okay?" He held out his hand to seal the deal.

"Done," I told him, shaking his hand and looking him in the eye. "But since we're being totally truthful with each other, I've gotta tell you—I don't buy that story about why you quit. Nobody gets that good at something and quits cold turkey 'cause they realize it's not a good way to meet girls and their stomach hurts. Why did you really quit?"

"Think what you want to think," he said. "I'm going to bed. Good night."

"Good night, Grandmaster. Can I call you that now?"

"Never, ever," he told me emphatically as he walked back into the house. And just before the screen door slammed I heard him mutter, "Good night, Patzer-face."

4

When a girl can look beautiful streaked with pond scum, you know she's dangerous. Her name was Britney, she was wearing waders and carrying a net, and her long brown hair was tucked up into a cap so it wouldn't drag in the murky waters of Grimwald Pond. "Hey, are you ready for some high-quality goo?" she asked, walking up to me and depositing a netful of sludge in my glass beaker.

Grimwald had been the first headmaster of Loon Lake Academy a hundred years ago. A photo of him hangs in the library near the reference section, a serious-looking man with a bushy mustache and a glare on his face that says: "Study harder and keep your big mouth shut." According to the dates under the photo he was headmaster for almost a quarter of a century, so he probably deserved something better than getting his name on this fetid pond.

"Collectors, scoop with the nets, don't jab with them," Mr.

Cady, our bio teacher, urged, walking up and down the long line of kids like a general appraising his troops. "Try to pre-serve the sedimentary logic of the ecosystem. Surveyors, be vigilant. What you dismiss as a wood chip may in fact be something truly remarkable. Recorders, please write legibly."

I was a surveyor, knee-deep in pond water, holding a big glass vial in one hand and a magnifying glass in the other. Britney was a collector. In addition to her netful of silt and ooze, she had managed to collect a long streak of orange-brown mud that ran from her hairline down past her wide blue eyes, an inch to the right of her cute nose, and terminated on a level with her puffy and highly sensual lips.

"Thanks," I told her, swishing her sample around in my water-filled vial and studying it through the magnifying glass. We had been in the same bio class for seven months, and even worked together as lab partners on occasion, but we had never stood together in a muddy pond before.

"You're welcome," she replied with a little smile. "This is disgusting, isn't it?"

"I don't think we're going to find much except mud and crud," I said. "Maybe an old shoe if we get real lucky."

"I kind of hope I don't find anything in here," she told me, peering down. "Even an old shoe sounds pretty gross." I ex-pected her to trudge deeper into the pond, but Mr. Cady had moved on down the line so no one was watching us. She lin-gered, took a step closer, and surprised me by saying: "I hear from Brad that you're going to New York this weekend."

I had e-mailed Brad the good news right after my conversation with Dad on the back porch. I nodded and tried to sound casual about it. She had never mentioned her senior boyfriend to me before. Come to think of it, in seven months of being in the same class, we had never discussed anything about our personal lives—not that I had much of a personal life. "Yeah, it should be, um, interesting."

"I know you guys will win," she said. "Brad is such a strong player. And Eric never loses at anything either." Her words sounded like such rah-rah girlfriend drivel that I almost dismissed her as a dumb and starry-eyed cheerleader for a jerk. But I couldn't help wondering if on some deeper level she wasn't really poking fun at Brad, and maybe even expressing a little sadness at being bound to these two arrogant big shots.

I wanted to ask her why a nice fourteen-year-old girl would date an eighteen-year-old jerk—even if he was handsome and successful—and why her parents would let her. But instead, I looked right into her glistening blue eyes and said: "Well, I'll probably lose every game. But it'll still be fun to go to New York with my dad."

She looked a little surprised. If she was hanging around Brad and Eric she probably never heard them express doubts about winning anything. "Oh, don't worry about screwing up," she told me. "Brad was telling me about the tournament. Each team has to have six players to enter, but for every round they only count the scores of the top five. So even if you lose every game, it's no problem. What's the matter?"

I stood there, nodding very slightly. Of course, that was

why they had invited me. They didn't care about my score—they were after my dad so they could have five superstrong players for each round. "Nothing," I told her. And then, trying to keep the bitterness out of my voice, I said: "You have mud on your face."

"Really? Yuck."

"Don't worry about it. It's just pond scum."

She gave me a curious look. "Did I make you feel bad telling you that only five players counted in each round? I thought you knew."

"I do now."

For a moment her face softened. "Sorry. The way Brad put it, it seemed like everyone was on the same page."

"I think you'd better collect some more mud," I told her. "There's nothing in this sample but silt."

Instead of walking away, Britney stepped yet closer. I could smell her lilac perfume over the stench of pond muck. "I think it's sweet that you want to go to New York with your dad. Would you do me a favor, Daniel?" she asked. "I'm wearing these waterproof gloves. Would you wipe the mud off for me?"

"Off your face?"

"Yup."

I swallowed. "With what?"

"Your hand."

I looked back at her and heard myself mumble: "Okay. Right or left?"

She giggled. "Whichever's cleanest."

I stuck the magnifying glass into my back pocket, handle first, and reached toward her hesitantly. The fingers of my right hand touched the side of her face.

"Go on, wipe it off," she said. "I don't bite."

I wiped the mud off, which meant gently stroking down the side of her face. She tilted her head slightly and smiled back a little playfully at me.

I reluctantly pulled my fingers away and took a breath. "It's all off," I said.

"Thanks, Daniel," she replied. "I may be coming to New York this weekend with my mom, so we may meet up with you guys for dinner. And you know what?"

"What?" I asked.

"I think you might just surprise yourself and win a game or two," she told me. "I bet you're a lot better than you know."

Then she turned and waded back into Grimwald Pond, her scoop net poised for the next interesting specimen that swam her way.

5

When I finished my homework on Thursday night and walked out into the living room, Dad was watching the news, but he was really waiting for me. He switched off the TV and said, "Where's your chess set?"

"Need to brush up?" I asked.

"I want to see if I still remember how to set the pieces up," he told me without a smile.

I got the purple sack and the green-and-white-checked board and handed them over. He unrolled the board and dumped the sack of pieces out onto it and started setting up the white side. I probably should have helped him by setting up the black pieces, but I couldn't stop myself from watching him.

He had the strangest look on his face, as if he were returning to a place where something beautiful but also terrible had happened to him long ago. I got the feeling he had been absolutely positive he would never visit this place again. He almost seemed to be climbing onto the board himself and rubbing shoulders with the pieces so that he could exchange small talk with the pawns and salute the king and climb the crenellated parapets of the rooks. When he picked up a knight, his hand trembled.

"You okay?" I asked him. "Something wrong with the knight?"

His hand had frozen for a moment, with the knight suspended in midair. He was holding the piece by its long equine neck, and I saw his thumb trace down the length of the plastic horse as if stroking its mane. "It's the only piece that can move at the beginning of a game," he told me softly.

"I never realized that," I said.

"The only one that can jump over others." He placed it almost reverently on the board. "Since chess was invented in India, more than a thousand years ago, it's the only piece whose role and movement have never changed at all."

"They don't teach us much about the history of chess in our club," I told him. "But I guess each piece has something unique about it."

He placed the white queen next to the king. "When they first cooked up the game, the king was a scholarly, wise Indian emperor—much too refined to do much fighting himself. What we call the queen was a male war minister who stood near and advised him. The Spanish later turned the piece into a powerful woman, probably to honor the Virgin Mary, or perhaps because women can be so dangerous."

I thought of Britney and how she had hurt my feelings and then reduced me to a babbling idiot when she asked me to wipe the mud off her face. "You can say that again," I muttered. "No wonder they can move so far in so many different directions."

His white pieces and pawns were ready now, and he set up the black pieces and then leaned back and surveyed the board. There was an expression on his face that I had never seen before—a dangerous sharpness, a knife-blade-like keenness. He was a gentle man, but peering down at the chess pieces through his thick glasses he looked downright nasty. "Do you have any idea what chess really is, Daniel?"

"A game? A pastime?" He shook his head and I tried again. "A three-dimensional timed logic test?"

"War," he told me. "Two armies facing each other on a battlefield, fighting to the death."

"That's one way to think about it."

"There's no other way. It's war and annihilation, pure and simple. When you capture a piece, you're killing it. When you capture the enemy king, his whole army is put to the sword."

"That's a pretty bloodthirsty interpretation," I said. "I prefer to think of it as a logic test."

"Logic test be damned," he grunted, and took a few fast breaths. His fingers had folded into fists and I could see how tense he was and how hard he was trying to relax. I wondered what was making him so nervous. "Listen," he said, "I made the hotel reservation at the Palace Royale. We're sharing a standard room. Twin beds. No frills. It's still more than two hundred a night."

"We could stay at home and drive back and forth," I suggested.

"No. The opening round is on Friday night, and the first Saturday round starts early. If we're gonna do this, let's stay in Manhattan and do it right."

"A standard room will be fine," I told him. "I don't care if I have to sleep on the floor." I tried to come up with something positive, to make him look a little happier. "Maybe we'll win first prize. It's ten thousand dollars, Dad. Our share of that would be more than three grand."

"I wouldn't count on that," he said.

"Brad and Eric are strong players," I pointed out, "and so are their dads. And I know you haven't played in years, but you were a grandmaster. So we probably have as good a shot as anyone."

"Aren't you forgetting somebody?" he asked. "What about you?"

I was very tempted to tell him about the five-player-a-round rule, and that they had only invited the two of us to add his score to their own totals. But instead I said: "Sure, I might have a strong tournament, too. You can never tell."

"No, you can't," he agreed, taking off his glasses and starting to polish them on his shirt, so that he was looking away from me when he added softly, "Daniel, you may hear something at the tournament about me."

"What kind of something?"

He was still looking down at his glasses and not at me. "The chess community is small. People hang around for years. They remember things they should have forgotten."

"You mean I may hear something bad about you?"

He glanced up at me, and there was a clear warning in his eyes. "If you do hear anything, I want you to remember it happened a long time ago. I was a very different person back then."

"Sure," I said. "Look, I'm the one who got you into this. Whatever happened in the past is history. But do you want to give me a heads-up about what I may hear, just so I can prepare myself to ignore it and forget it?"

"No," he said, "I'd rather not. Let's play."

"Against you? You're a grandmaster."

"Then I'll give you white."

He turned the board around so that the white pieces were in front of me. "Go ahead, son," he said. "Bring it on."

So I tried to bring it. I know other kids wrestle their fathers, or race them, or play one-on-one basketball against them, but we had never even arm-wrestled before. This was the first time that I could remember my father and me going full tilt at each other in friendly combat.

I say "friendly" because we started out amicably enough, smiling and making small talk—and we were playing in the warmth and comfort of our own living room. Also, there was nothing at stake—no money, no trophies, not even rating points.

But the underlying vibe of the game didn't stay friendly for long. I'd never thought of my father as particularly aggressive, but when he sat facing me at the chessboard that evening, his shoulders hunched slightly forward, his fingers knitted tightly together on the table while he scrutinized the pieces and sometimes glanced up at me, his intensity was tangible, and he seemed formidable and bent on annihilation.

He also talked trash. Chess is supposed to be a silent game, and if someone annoys you with conversation during a tournament, you can raise your hand and wave over an official who will tell your opponent to zip his lip. But the only person I could have appealed to was my mom, who was futzing around the kitchen baking brownies and occasionally throwing surprised but pleased glances at us, as if to say, "Look at the two of you boys, having fun together! You should both be packing for your big trip tomorrow, but I'm not going to break this magical father-son moment."

I played my usual king's pawn opening and he muttered, "Really?" and then, after he'd slammed his own king's pawn forward two squares: "It only gets worse from here." Soon he was on the edge of falling into an opening trap with a ridiculous nickname—the Fried Liver.

I felt a little bad for him, because when I get someone into the Fried Liver I always destroy him. But at the same time, his aggressiveness seemed to be contagious, or maybe it was just the father-son rivalry kicking into high gear.

I wanted to beat him and shut his trash-talking mouth. I wanted to put his army to the sword. "Maybe you have been away from chess a little too long," I muttered, springing my trap.

He glared back at me for half a second and then made an unexpected move, and I soon found that I was the one trapped. I wiggled and flailed, but in five moves I was hopelessly lost, and I soon knocked over my king. "You rule, Grandmaster. For now."

He held out his hand.

I reached out and took it. I couldn't remember ever shaking my father's hand quite this way before. We had, of course, shaken hands many times in the past, but always for formal occasions, when our handshakes had a clear purpose. This wasn't a congratulatory shake, or a consolatory shake—it was the handshake of two buddies who have just done something fun or, at least, something that's supposed to be fun. He held the grip a few seconds longer than necessary and looked into my eyes. "Don't be pissed off."

"I'll get you next time."

He released my hand. "You do realize that I didn't beat you at chess?" he asked.

I looked back at him. "That wasn't chess?"

"Nope," he said. "Chess is two minds doing fair battle. Chess is forcing your opponent to outthink you strategically and creatively. I didn't have to think at all in that game because you never got me off a very well-known line. Why on earth do you play that opening?"

"It was the first opening in the book," I told him. "Most of the kids play it—at least the beginners."

"That," he said, "is exactly why you *shouldn't* play it. Especially against someone like me. The Giuoco Piano has been around for five hundred years. It's been analyzed to death. And it's sheer suicide to try to trap someone with the Fried Liver unless you know the Traxler Counter Gambit and all its subvariations."

"Guess I'll have to study harder."

"Forget it," he told me. "There are lots of kids out there who study chess openings for two hours a day. I know because I was one of them. If you play the main lines of the most common openings against them, they'll beat the pants off you twenty times in a row without ever having to think of an original move."

"So what should I do?" I asked.

"Play something sound but obscure. Choose an opening where you'll get a solid position after ten moves, and they'll soon be off the book and forced to think for themselves. Suddenly that giant advantage they have—of hundreds of hours studying opening theory and traps—will be gone. They'll have to come up with their own original moves, which means you'll be meeting evenly on the field of mind combat—and you'll have a legitimate chance."

"The tournament starts tomorrow night," I told him. I glanced at my watch. "Twenty-one hours and counting. There's no time for me to start learning new openings."

Dad hesitated a long beat, and then he began to set up the pieces again, but this time he didn't do it slowly. His hands moved so fast that the pawns and knights and bishops became a black-and-white blur. He lifted his palms and they were all in place, as if he had conjured them. "Okay, Daniel," he said, "pay close attention. This is where we start."

6

"Don't forget underwear," my mother said as I finished tossing clothes into a duffel bag.

"I'm not planning on wearing any," I told her. "Underwear's unlucky. I play better without it."

She looked at me. "You're kidding, right?"

"I packed plenty of clean underwear, Mom," I promised her. "And if I run out, I'm sure they sell it near our hotel. They probably sell socks, too, somewhere in Manhattan."

She closed the door and lowered her voice to a whisper. "Take care of your father."

"Take care of him how?"

"I don't know," she said. "He never has trouble sleeping, but he was up for hours last night, twisting and turning. Then, after midnight, he got up and tiptoed out of the bedroom."

"Midnight snack?"

She shook her head. "I followed him."

"You sneak."

"Spying is part of my job as a wife and mother."

"Where did he go?"

"The study," she said. "He switched on my computer."

"Your laptop? I wonder why."

"I bet because it's newer," she said, "so it's the only one that has a chess application."

"You saw him playing the computer?"

"Yes," she admitted. "I peeked in the door and he was sitting at the desk, his hands folded, his eyes burning at the screen. Daniel, I've never seen him look like that."

"Like what?" I asked.

"Like he wanted to strangle someone."

"The computer must have been beating him," I guessed. "I think you can set it right up to master level, and maybe even to grandmaster strength. The new programs are really powerful. No one in my club can beat them."

She shrugged. "I couldn't tell who was winning. But he was talking to it. Insulting it. Calling it names. Gizmo. Dolt. Screwhead."

"Screwhead?" I repeated with a smile. "Really?"

"It's not funny. He was threatening it. I've never heard your father ever threaten anyone, and . . ."

Dad's voice drifted in from the living room. "Daniel, are you packed? We've got to hit the road."

"Just getting clean underwear," I shouted back. I could see how concerned Mom was. "Don't worry," I told her. "He's just a very competitive chess player."

She put her hand on my arm. "I am worried. I thought it

would be good for you two to share an activity. But there's something going on here that I don't understand and I don't like. He's not a young man, your father, and he has high blood pressure."

"Not anymore," I said. "He got it down and under control."

"He got it down with pills," she said. "I want you to watch him and—"

Dad opened the door. "What are you two up to?"

"I was just wishing my baby good luck," Mom told him, and kissed me on the cheek. "Don't forget to call. As many times a day as you like. Kate and I want to hear all the exciting news."

"Actually, I couldn't care less about the chess mess," Kate called out from the living room. "But the salient point—do you like that vocabulary word, Mom?—the salient point here is that Daniel's getting to go on an expensive trip to New York and I'm not. All the parenting books recommend fairness and equality between kids, so the only fair thing would be if I got to go on a shopping trip next weekend, and I've already picked out some stores . . ."

"The salient point is that you might use our absence to stop worrying about parenting books and start worrying about your history project," Dad told her. "Now get out of the way before I run you over with my suitcase." He headed out into the living room, and I hoisted up my duffel bag and followed him.

"Are you threatening your own daughter?" Kate asked,

and then screamed and jumped to one side as Dad ran at her with his rolling suitcase, the wheels squeaking across the wooden floor.

I gave Mom a kiss and a reassuring hug. "Don't worry about a thing," I told her. And then in a softer voice: "What could go wrong at a chess tournament?"

She looked back at me and raised her eyebrows, as if to ask, "How should I know?" I followed Dad out the door, down the steps, to our car.

We headed out of town and were soon on a wide-open four-lane highway, speeding eastward at seventy miles per hour while Friday afternoon commuters endured stop-and-go traffic in the westbound lanes. Driving seemed to relax Dad a little bit. He opened his window a crack, put on some jazz, and then glanced at me and said, "So, tell me about the rest of our team."

"The Chisolms and the Kinneys."

"The boys are friends of yours?"

"Not exactly friends. They're both seniors."

"It was nice of them to ask a freshman along. I take it they're good kids?"

"They're good at a lot of things," I answered carefully.

"Like what?"

"Brad's the captain of the swim team and holds the school records for several distances. Eric's the senior class president and valedictorian."

"World beaters," Dad muttered.

"You could say that."

He heard the edge in my tone and turned down the jazz. "You don't like them?"

"We're not exactly best chums."

"Then why the heck are we doing this?" he demanded.

"Because they invited us," I told him.

"Who cares?"

"I do. They never even talked to me before."

"Do you mean to say," Dad asked, "that we're going to all this trouble and expense—driving to New York and playing in a three-day tournament—to get on the good side of two stuck-up jerks who you don't even like?"

I nodded. "That pretty much sums it up."

"Well, that's . . . screwy," Dad said.

"It is screwy," I agreed. "But you might as well hear the rest of it."

"Sure," Dad said, "since I reserved a hotel room—which it's now too late to cancel—and I paid the nonrefundable three-hundred-dollar registration fee, this seems like a good time for me to hear the truth."

"The truth is they think I'm a terrible player, as well as a social zero, but they couldn't care less about that."

"They'd better care about you," Dad said. "It's a team event, right? With six players, we all have to do well to have a chance."

"Wrong," I muttered, finally admitting the embarrassing truth to him. "In each round they'll count the top five scores out of six. Since there are five rounds, the best possible team score is five wins per round for a total of twenty-five."

Dad switched off the jazz and gripped the steering wheel a little tighter. He looked quite angry. "I figured they invited me as a ringer, but you're saying they've completely discounted you already, and you're just window dressing?"

"Correct," I admitted. "They want to win this thing, and you're their ace in the hole. Grandmasters don't grow on trees. I'm just along for the ride."

"Why didn't you tell me this before?" he demanded.

I shrugged. "I thought if you found out you might not come."

"I'll fix them," Dad said. "I'll lose every game on purpose."

"Don't do that. Please."

"Why not?" he demanded. "They deserve it."

I was silent for a while, and then I spoke in a soft voice, staring straight ahead at the spire of the Empire State Building that had just become visible in the distance, poking up across the Hudson River. "I'm not exactly the most popular kid at school," I confessed.

"Who is?" Dad asked.

"Chisolm and Kinney are superstars," I told him. Dad tried to point out something, but I waved for him to be silent, and he took the hint. "In fact, I'm kind of low man on the totem pole in a lot of areas," I went on. "You might have been too busy with tax season to notice, but my midterm grades weren't great, I didn't make the freshman basketball team, and cute girls aren't exactly lining up to date me."

"All perfectly normal for a high school freshman," Dad noted. "Listen, don't be too hard on yourself. You've got plenty of time. You're a great kid." He tried to put his hand on my shoulder again, but I shrugged it off. "I *was* busy during tax season, but I should have taken more of an interest in how you were doing," he admitted.

"Let's not have too many mushy moments," I muttered.

"Fine. But do you hate this private school?" he asked. "Did your mother and I make a mistake sending you there?"

"No, it's a fine school," I told him. "And there are some nice kids. I just haven't made friends with them yet. Doing well in this chess tournament with these two—world beaters— wouldn't hurt my popularity. And I'd like to win at something just once. Okay?"

"I still think it's screwy, but okay," Dad said. "If I can help you out and raise your stock, I'll do my best. The truth is I don't think I could lose a chess game on purpose, even if I wanted to." He drove for a while in silence. "What about the fathers of these boys?" he asked uncomfortably. "I assume the apples didn't drop far from the rich and conceited trees?"

"Dr. Chisolm is a surgeon," I told him. "He spoke to our chess club once. He's a little on the competitive side."

"What about Kinney?"

"Owns his own hedge fund. The school pool is named after him. Eric says he's an expert player, and if he has a strong tournament he might make the master norm like his son."

"Great," Dad said. "Terrific." He was silent as we headed down the long ramp to the Lincoln Tunnel. Finally he said: "Tell you what, Daniel."

"What?"

"We'll do this, because it's too late to stop, but the only way it makes sense is if we do it for us."

"How do you mean?" I asked. We paid a toll and drove into the long tunnel beneath the Hudson River.

"Well, we don't get away on father-son trips to New York all that often," he pointed out.

"Like never."

"Right. So let's try to have some laughs and good times together."

"Sounds fine to me," I told him. "And, since we're being totally honest, I know you didn't want to do this. Sorry I got you into it."

"It still might be marginally better than going on a shopping trip with your sister," Dad grunted, and then we passed a dividing line on the wall of the tunnel and a sign announced that we had entered New York City.

1

The Palace Royale Hotel was smack in the middle of Midtown, a gleaming new tower of glass and steel that rose high above Broadway. We drove past it and parked the car in a garage two blocks away. "Thirty bucks a day," Dad muttered, tucking the garage ticket away in his wallet and shaking his head. "We should have taken the train."

I didn't get into Manhattan all that often, and the pace of the city was as dizzying as I remembered—people exploded off curbs when lights changed to green, insane taxi drivers honked at one another and nearly clipped pedestrians as they wove in and out of traffic, while crowds surged outside the glass doors of Broadway theaters. I hurried along next to my dad, listening to the sounds of the city and inhaling its scents: sizzling meat from a parked gyro truck, steam hissing up through a subway grate, and a lady in a fur coat sashaying ahead of us in four-inch heels that *click-clicked* off the sidewalk as if she were stabbing it with each purposeful step.

A doorman in a top hat stood outside the Palace Royale Hotel, helping people in and out of cabs, which he summoned with earsplitting blasts on a silver whistle. "Okay," Dad said to me, "ready?"

"As I'll ever be."

"Then let the madness begin," he said, and we spun our way in through the revolving door.

The lobby was brightly carpeted, with a chandelier glistening high above. A sign near the check-in desk read WELCOME CHESS PLAYERS. I could pick out dozens of them—sharp-eyed kids clutching sets and clocks, many of them nose-deep into chess books, as if in the next hour, before round one started, they were going to uncover a key secret that would mean the difference between victory and defeat.

Their dads hovered around them, and it was easy to spot the father-son resemblances—the hawk-nosed dad and the eagle-beaked son; the hyper kid who couldn't stand still and his nervous dad who paced from side to side at the check-in line like a caged tiger.

We reached the front desk and a pretty clerk asked for my dad's name. "Pratzer," he said. "You should have a reservation for a standard room, two twin beds."

"That's been changed," she informed him. "You've been upgraded to a suite and moved to our club floor."

"I don't want a suite," Dad told her.

"Oh yes you do," she replied with a knowing smile. "Thirteen hundred square feet, two luxury bedrooms, and a living area with spectacular views."

"But I didn't ask for that," Dad pointed out. He looked a little embarrassed and lowered his voice. "I don't want to pay for that."

"Not to worry. It's already been taken care of."

He stared back at her. "By who?"

She studied her monitor. "Randolph J. Kinney. He's on the club floor, too, right next to you. Here are your key cards. Suite 2207. Enjoy your stay, Mr. Pratzer."

We took the elevator up to the twenty-second floor. "I can't let a stranger pay for my room upgrade." Dad fumed.

"Why not?" I asked. "He owns a hedge fund."

"I don't care if he owns his own bank."

"He probably does," I said. "Let's check out the suite before you give it up."

The elevator reached the twenty-second floor and we got out. The club floor was elegant and silent—a welcome change from the crowded lobby. "Not bad," I said.

"Don't get used to it," Dad warned me. "I'm gonna get us downgraded right after our first round is over."

We opened the door to suite 2207 and I sucked in a breath. The marble entry hall led to a spacious living area, which featured two leather couches, an enormous flat-screen TV, and floor-to-ceiling windows with stunning views westward over Manhattan rooftops all the way to New Jersey. The sun was going down over the Hudson, and it gave the mile-wide river a dark purple tinge. The two bedrooms had king-size beds and their own TVs, the master bathroom had a Jacuzzi, and there was a fruit basket on the desk with the words WELCOME GRANDMASTER PRATZER—THE MANAGE-MENT.

"If you downgrade us from this room, I might have to kill you," I told my dad.

He was contemplating the fruit basket. "How could they possibly know I was a grandmaster . . . ?"

A loud knock sounded on our door, and I went to open it. A tall, handsome, and athletic-looking man in slacks and a sports coat was standing there, grinning and looking past me. "Is that you, Grandmaster? Randolph Kinney." He stepped into our suite and a second later he was pumping my dad's right hand in a grip that made my father visibly wince. "How do you like the spread?"

"It's great," I chimed in before my father could answer.

"Bloody hell, I think you guys got the better view," Mr. Kinney said with a laugh.

"I can't let you pay for this," my father told him, extracting his hand from the viselike grip and tucking it into his pocket to give it a chance to heal.

"I appreciate that offer, Morris, I really do," Randolph said. "But this one's on me. I thought our team should all be to-gether. It's the least I can do to thank you for coming. It isn't every day that I get to play on a team with a real, authentic grandmaster. It's an honor, a real honor. I'm humbled."

My father looked back at him, speechless.

Randolph Kinney turned to me. "And a big hello also to

the grandmaster's son," he announced, stepping over and holding out his hand. "Daniel, right?"

I backed up half a step and hesitated, but there seemed to be no way of avoiding this. I reached out tentatively and he seized my palm as if he intended to wring blood out of it. "We're gonna win this thing," he assured me, grinning and doing his best to crush all the small bones in my right hand. "We're gonna kick butt. We're going to slay them. Right?"

"I hope so," I gasped.

"There's no 'hope so' about it," he said, and for a moment his voice had an edge to it. "When we play, we play to win. And we've got the goods!"

He released my hand and glanced at his watch. "The first round starts in forty minutes. Let's have a team meeting in my suite in ten minutes, and we'll all go down to the tournament together. We're in 2206. Grandmaster, given that you have the highest rating, I think you should deliver the team prayer."

"The team prayer?" my dad echoed.

"Keep it short and sweet." Randolph was halfway to the door. "An honor, Grandmaster, a real honor," he said. "Oh, and don't worry about dinner after the round. I booked us into a little Tribeca steak house that I know. We need to eat some red meat after we draw first blood." Then he was gone.

My dad threw his arms into the air. "Daniel, this is preposterous. I knew this was going to happen. Chess tournaments lead you right down the rabbit hole. We should go get our car, drive back home, and wake up in our normal beds before the world tilts any more, which believe me it will. Let's get out of here now."

I glanced at the clock. "Eight minutes and counting," I told him. "If I were you, Dad, I'd be working on the team prayer."

My father wouldn't come out of the bedroom. *"Dad, we're late for the team meeting. They've already called twice,"* I shouted. There was no answer from inside. I stepped closer to the door. "Pop?" I opened his bedroom door a crack. "Are you okay?"

I hesitated and stepped inside. There was no sign of him in the bedroom, and then I felt cold air and saw that one window was open.

Then I heard something from his bathroom. It was a loud, unpleasant heaving sound. It let up and then came again even louder. I ran to the door and yanked it open and saw him on his knees, retching into the toilet. I stepped over to him. "Dad, are you okay? Should I call a doctor?"

He flushed the toilet and struggled to his feet, looking a little pale. "Don't worry," he gasped. He ran some cold water and wiped his face and toweled off. "This is normal . . . for me . . . before a tournament starts."

"You don't look so good," I told him. "You can't play in this condition . . ."

"The first round starts in twenty-five minutes," he responded, checking his watch. He took a gulp of cold tap water, gargled, and spat it out. "Let's go." As we walked through the bedroom, he paused to close the window. "Just needed some fresh air," he told me. "I always feel claustrophobic before round one."

He led me out into the living area, walking more purposefully now, face tight but resigned, back straight and head held high—like a man marching bravely to his own execution. Seeing Dad on his knees, retching his guts out, had made me realize for the first time how torturous this must be for him. "Are you sure you're *really* okay?" I asked. "Because if you're sick and need to pull out of the tournament, I'm sure they'll understand."

"I'm sure they won't understand," he told me as we left our suite. "We're in this now, Daniel, and the only thing to do is to keep going forward. Ours is not to reason why; ours is just to do and die." He raised his right fist and rapped firmly on the Kinneys' door.

Brad opened the door. "You're late, Patzer-face." Then he saw my dad and said, "Oh . . ."

"I'm Grandmaster Patzer-face," my father told him, holding out his right hand. "And let me guess. You must be our team captain."

"We don't have a team captain," Brad replied, looking a little uncomfortable as he shook my father's hand.

"We do now," Dad told him. "I'm appointing you captain. Which means you're in charge of team morale and making sure that all team members treat one another with the proper respect. *Got it?*"

Brad looked like he was on the verge of saying something rude back to my father, but then his own dad appeared behind him.

"You're seven minutes late, Morris," Mr. Kinney scolded.

"Yes, well, I was strategizing and working on that team prayer, and I also had to puke," my father told him.

For a moment, the hedge fund king was knocked off balance. "What? Are you okay?"

"Never better," Dad told him, walking by him into their suite. "Where's the rest of our team?"

"Over here, behind the couch," a voice shouted.

We stepped to the long leather couch and saw that behind it Eric Chisolm and his father were doing sit-ups. Dr. Chisolm was a wiry man with closely cropped graying hair and no visible body fat. "One hundred and ninety-nine, two hundred," he counted and stood up.

Eric stayed on his back on the rug.

"You must be Morris Pratzer," the spry doctor said. "Sam Chisolm. My son and I were just doing our cardio warm-up sets. Stand up, Eric."

Eric was still lying on his back, holding his abdomen and breathing hard. Watching father and son, I started to suspect that Eric was the school's biggest overachiever because his father was the world's biggest ballbuster.

"Don't let us stop you," Dad said.

"We're done," the surgeon assured him, taking his own pulse. "Two hundred really gets the blood flowing. On your feet, son. Get vertical."

Eric struggled to his knees, looking as if his large intestine had been ripped out.

"Here's your kit," Randolph Kinney said, hurrying up to us and handing out canvas tote bags. "I had an assistant at my firm put this together for us. Team shirts, score pads, pencils, bottled water."

I took out the shirt. It said MIND CRIPPLERS. I pulled it on over my shirt, and my dad and I exchanged looks.

"We didn't come here to meet future pen pals," Mr. Kinney told us, picking up on our dubious expressions. "We came to conquer."

I glanced at my dad. He shared the belief that chess was war. He should have been nodding. Instead, he was watching Brad's dad carefully.

"There are more than four hundred players in this tournament," Mr. Kinney continued. "Seventy-two teams—and at the end there will be one left standing. That one team will be us. We need to start fast and come away from the first round with five points. Anything less will be *unacceptable*."

"Six points would be even better," Dr. Chisolm chipped in. "Even though only five will count. There's medical evidence that winning is addictive. Let's learn to expect success."

Mr. Kinney nodded. "Expect success. I like that. Let's make it our team motto." He glanced at his expensive watch.

"Seventeen minutes till start time. We've got to head down soon. Grandmaster, please deliver the Mind Cripplers' team prayer. One knee, gentlemen."

It seemed silly, but when Randolph Kinney gave an order, he expected it to be followed. All of us got down on one knee on the plush blue rug in his hotel suite. "Link hands," he told us, and I found myself holding my father's left hand and Dr. Chisolm's right. Chisolm's fingers felt wiry and strong, and it occurred to me that this was a hand that had saved hundreds of lives. However intense the doctor was, he was a miracle worker who took very sick and dying people and fixed them and sent them back to their families. My father's hand felt soft and clammy and shook slightly. I gripped it tightly.

"A moment of silence, everyone," Mr. Kinney commanded. Something told me that many years ago he had played football for the Loon Lake Academy, and this pregame ritual was left over from his locker room memories. Then he nodded to my father. "Go ahead, Grandmaster."

My dad cleared his throat. It's interesting how you can know someone all your life but not have a clue how they're going to react in a new and totally freaky situation. Dad and I had never talked about religion, but I was pretty sure he was an atheist. I'd never heard him pray—even on a family trip to Mexico when our plane hit extreme turbulence and I started making pleas to the almighty, he had kept quiet.

Even if my dad did believe in God, he's a fair and logical man, and I was positive that he wouldn't lead us in the kind of team prayer Mr. Kinney wanted him to give. If there was a God, my father wouldn't think it was fair to ask an all-powerful being to intercede for us against another team.

Dad was quiet for a long moment, and then he surprised me by shutting his eyes and intoning in a low and serious voice: "O Lord, who looks down upon us and sees everything we do, this is Morris Pratzer giving you a shout-out from suite 2206 of the Palace Royale Hotel." I suspected he was poking fun at the whole absurd situation, but at the same time his tone was solemn and he had a very serious look on his face. Mr. Kinney and Dr. Chisolm seemed to be buying it, at least for now.

"Lord," my father continued, "help us to be brave and strong and play well and conquer."

"Amen to that," Mr. Kinney muttered, glancing at his watch. "Fifteen minutes, Grandmaster."

Dad gave him a quick glance. "And let us be also aware of our own weaknesses." His voice quivered and for a moment my father's words sounded like a heartfelt prayer. "Let us not be blinded by false confidence. Help us to remember the great and small blunders we've made along the way." His voice dropped to a whisper: "I, who loved chess as a boy and haven't played a game in thirty years, humbly ask for your special guidance and mercy."

I couldn't understand why he used the word "mercy."

Mr. Kinney was staring at my father, surprised and not pleased. "*Thirty years, Morris?* I hope you've been practicing on the side, because that's a heck of a long time . . ."

Dad's voice swelled, drowning Mr. Kinney out. "Most important, Lord, we thank you for the blessing of playing in this tournament with our sons. Perhaps we have been too busy and have neglected them. Maybe we have hidden ourselves from them. Perhaps we have not shown them our love." I couldn't be sure, but I think his hand clenched my own just a bit tighter. "Grant us the wisdom to know how fleeting time is, so that we can cherish this precious weekend together. Winning is important, but the love of a father for his son is by far the greater blessing. Amen."

Mr. Kinney opened his mouth and I thought he was going to tell my dad that he was wrong, and that winning was the only goal here. Then his finger stroked the side of his cheek. I'm not sure, because he turned his head away, but I believe he might have dabbed away a tear. "Amen," he repeated in a low voice. "Well said, Morris."

"Amen," Dr. Chisolm echoed, springing to his feet like a mountain goat leaping off a rock. "No doubt about it, family love is the most important thing here. Now come on, Eric. Let's go slaughter them!"

9

The elevator doors opened to a mob scene. We stepped out onto the common area of the tournament floor where a crowd was clustered around large pairings sheets taped to the walls. Nervous fathers and sons jostled one another to try to get close enough to read what board they'd been assigned to and who they were supposed to play.

I wormed my way forward and finally made it close enough to find my name. This tournament would follow the Swiss System—in every round players would be matched against opponents who had the same win-loss record. In the first round, since everyone had zero wins and zero losses, higher-rated players had been matched against lower-rated ones. I was supposed to play a guy named Liu Hong, who was rated more than three hundred points higher than me and who would most probably crush me.

I scanned the list for my dad's name and saw that he was

matched against an expert named Marciano on board three. Experts are rated just below masters—which means they really know what they're doing. A grandmaster wouldn't normally have much trouble beating an expert, but I wondered how Dad would fare in such a tough first game after not playing for three decades.

I forced my way out of the scrum and looked around for my father. He had wandered over to where the tournament rankings were posted. A series of computer printouts listed all four hundred and thirty-two players in order of their Chess Federation ratings, from highest to lowest. At the very top were five grandmasters. Morris W. Pratzer—with an asterisk next to his name because he hadn't played for so long—was third, beneath Grandmaster Salvador Sanchez and Grandmaster George Liszt. I was ranked near the bottom, but there were several dozen players beneath me. Most of those players were just starting out and didn't yet have ratings.

Dad didn't notice me walk up—he was studying the printout intently. I stepped next to him. "You're pretty high up there, Killer."

He shrugged. "Don't get hung up on ratings . . ."

"By God, is that you, Morry?" a deep voice boomed from behind us. I turned and saw a burly man in what looked like a red flannel hunter's shirt, with an untrimmed black beard that tumbled to his chest. Everything about him was big, from his loud voice to his ponderous stomach to his hands that seemed as large as baseball mitts. "I couldn't believe it when

I saw your name. But it really is you, isn't it? I figured you had died back in the nineties."

"Hello, George," my father said, and I noticed that despite the fact that they obviously knew each other from long ago, neither of them seemed inclined to shake hands.

"And this must be your son."

"Daniel, this is George Liszt. An old . . ." My father searched for the right word.

"Rival?" the big man suggested with a slight smile. "And admirer. I was always a big fan of your father's, Daniel." He smiled at me, but it was an ironic smile, as if he was signaling to me that his words had a hidden and quite opposite meaning. "He was the best of us," Grandmaster Liszt told me. "No one ever played like him . . . with such all-consuming zeal . . ."

"Enough, George," my father warned. "Where's your own son?"

"Already at his board," Liszt said. "At least I hope he is. His teammates call him the 'Ghost' because he's impossible to find between rounds. He's addicted to all sports and he just sits in our bedroom flipping through sports channels . . ."

A buzzer sounded from inside the ballroom, and a voice announced over loudspeakers: "Round one will begin in five minutes. Chess players, find your boards."

My father put his arm around my shoulder. "Come."

We had to walk around the walrus of a grandmaster to get to the ballroom doors, and for a moment George Liszt blocked our way. "Best of luck, Morry," he rumbled. "I hope you find some of the old magic." He had developed a mocking tone to go with his ironic smile. "But not too much of it."

"Good luck to you, too," Dad growled through gritted teeth.

"A great pleasure meeting you, Daniel," Grandmaster Liszt told me. "You have some big shoes to fill. Maybe we'll run into each other again before we're done here and find the time for a little chat."

I shrugged as my father yanked me away toward the ballroom. Dad's head was down and his teeth were clenched so tightly it looked like he would grind his molars to powder. "Don't worry about it," I told him. "Whatever that guy's problem is, he's clearly a jerk."

"I should never have come," Dad murmured. "It was asking for trouble."

Side by side we walked through the gaping doors of the Palace Royale's grand ballroom, into a massive playing space that looked as big as a football field. Dad wasn't the only one feeling nervous. I gazed around and felt myself tense up. Hundreds of tables had been arranged in perfect rows and covered with white cloths. Chess pieces had been set up on boards and stood ready for action. The tables had numbers on their sides, and fathers and sons were wishing one another good luck and finding their places. I had played in a few club tournaments in New Jersey, but nothing on this vast scale.

I knew I wasn't a strong player, and I certainly hadn't studied chess theory night and day, so I didn't expect miracles. But now that I was here, I found myself hoping that I could do a little better than expected, especially with my father's help. After all, he was a grandmaster and I was his son. I had inherited his athletic ineptitude and some of his mathematical ability, so wasn't it possible that I also had some of his chess genes, if not genius? George Liszt's mocking words had hit home—something extra was expected of me.

"What board are you?" Dad asked.

"One-ninety-seven," I told him, which meant I must be near the back of the hall. "I'm playing a Chinese guy rated much higher. He's probably going to crush me, but don't worry about it. This is your show. You must be up on the stage." The top five tables were on a kind of raised dais at the very front of the ballroom, near a dozen enormous trophies that glittered in the bright light.

Dad didn't head for the stage—he stayed right with me. "First of all, as I told you before, don't get hung up on ratings," he cautioned. "They mean less than you think, unless you believe in them and give them power. Just play carefully and you'll do fine." Dad pointed. "As for playing a Chinese guy, you got that wrong, too."

Looking down the long row of fathers and sons getting ready to square off against one another, I saw one teenage girl. She was seated at board 197. A short, pleasant-looking Chinese woman stood behind her, setting her chess clock.

"Two minutes," the voice boomed from the loudspeakers. *"Find your boards."*

"Go," I told my father. "I'll be all right." I didn't want him to be late. At chess tournaments, you have to make a certain number of moves in a set amount of time or you lose the game. Dad was out of practice, and I didn't want him to give away any precious minutes.

"I'll just come and get you settled," he said. "It's okay if I'm a minute or two late. I play quickly."

I walked over to the girl. She was reading a novel and totally ignoring her mother and the chess insanity all around her. On closer inspection, the book was *David Copperfield* by Charles Dickens, which we had just finished in our freshman English class. "Hi," I said. "I think we're playing each other in round one."

She finished a paragraph and stuck a bookmark in the novel, but she still didn't close it.

"Liu, *put away the book*," her mother commanded. "It's time to concentrate on chess."

"Worry about your own game," the girl told her mom in an irritated voice. Then she glanced up at me. She was wearing jeans and a light blue sweater, and she had tiny hoop earrings. Her hair hung down behind her in a long braid. "You're late," she said to me.

I sat down opposite her. "Actually, there are still two minutes left. I'm Daniel Patzer . . ." I caught myself and shot her a goofy grin. "I mean Pratzer."

"I know who you are," she said without smiling back. "I've already filled out both of our score sheets, since you seemed to have gotten lost."

"Liu," her mother urged, "make an effort to at least pretend to be polite."

Liu shot her mom an exasperated glare and then flashed me a fake smile and held out her hand. "Hi, Daniel. Where did you say you were from?"

I didn't know what to do so I shook her hand. It felt small and warm. "New Jersey," I told her. "Sorry to be late. We had a team meeting."

"Mind Cripplers," she said, reading my shirt. "That's a charming name."

"I didn't think it up," I responded, getting fed up with her attitude, "so chill out."

There was a momentary awkward silence. "I take it you're in the tournament, too?" Dad asked her mom. "I didn't know there was a mother-daughter bracket."

"I'll ignore the sexist implications to that," her mother said, and I saw where Liu got her prickliness. "As a matter of fact, there are no separate brackets. No one thought to make an official rule that it had to be just fathers and sons, so we're all in the same tournament. Anything a man can do, a woman can do better. I taught my daughter chess, and I'm playing at board thirty-five," she said proudly. "What about you?"

"Three," Dad told her.

Her eyebrows shot up. *What?*

"Let's go find our boards," Dad suggested, "and leave these two novices to their combat. Good luck, Daniel, and you too, young lady. No mercy."

The two of them walked off toward the front of the ballroom, and I was left alone with this fire-breathing dragon of a girl. The chessboard and the pieces were between us. The clock was on the right side of the board, waiting to be started. Liu stared at me, sizing me up—and then put her chin on her hands and leaned forward. "So, Daniel from New Jersey. Anything on your mind?"

"That's a good book," I said. "I just read it."

"It would be good if it wasn't so incredibly, unbelievably boring," Liu replied.

"I didn't find it boring at all," I told her. "In fact, I thought it was one of the best books I've ever read."

A man with a microphone walked out to the front of the dais. "On behalf of the tournament organizers, I'd like to welcome you all to the First Annual Father-Son National Championship. Before we begin, I have a special treat that I'm sure all our chess enthusiasts, young and old, will enjoy. Former World Champion Contender Arkady Shuvalovitch will say a few words. Arkady?" He paused and looked around. "Has anyone seen Arkady?"

"Can you believe this?" Liu muttered. Then she asked me, "So is your father really at board three or did he make that up?"

"He's there."

"So then . . . he's like a master?"

"No," I corrected her, "he's a grandmaster."

Liu took that in. "He taught you to play? Why aren't you better?"

I'm usually very shy around girls, but Liu was so rude that it relaxed me and freed me up to respond with some attitude of my own. "Actually, I didn't even know my dad played chess till a week ago," I told her. "And he never taught me a damned thing, not even how the pawns move."

She looked intrigued. "Really? That's kind of cool. Why not?"

She was making me angrier and angrier. "I don't have a clue," I told her. "But I don't think it's cool at all. And for what it's worth, you're wrong about *David Copperfield*. It's a great book, even if you can't appreciate it. And I wasn't even late— this stupid tournament hasn't even started because they can't find Former World Champion Contender Schmuck-a-vich. But other than that, it's been a real pleasure meeting you, Liu."

For a heartbeat she looked like she was about to smile. Then she caught herself, and her face tightened in anger. "Don't try to soften me up by flirting with me," she said.

"What? I'm not trying to flirt with you."

"Because I'm going to crush you."

"Probably," I nodded. "Who cares?"

"Not me," she said. "I was supposed to go to a concert with some friends, but my mom made me come."

"We're in the same boat," I told her. "I made my dad come. And now I regret it." Liu looked intrigued, and I surprised myself by adding: "He may be a grandmaster but he hasn't played in thirty years."

A schlubby-looking man in an ill-fitting black suit stumbled out onto the dais from a side door, blinked in the lights, and took the microphone. "I am Shuvalovitch," he said in heavily accented English. "Welcome, chess players, young and old, fathers and sons. As we say, chess is like a bridge. In order to get to the other side, you need to cross it. I wish good luck to everyone. Start your clocks."

"Utter nonsense, but what do you expect?" Liu muttered, reaching over to start the clock.

"I understood it clear as a bell," I told her. "Good luck, Liu. Don't fall off the bridge."

She couldn't help smiling as she reached out to make her first move, and it was an unexpectedly pretty smile. "I won't," she said. "I'm going to thrash you."

10

There is a moment at a chess tournament when the silence takes hold. Background noises continue—cars honk from outside, tournament officials pad up and down the rows, and there's the steady *whap-whap* of pieces being slammed down onto new squares. But a few minutes into a tournament, the mass concentration of the participants seems to knit together into a heavy blanket that dampens all peripheral sounds. Four hundred and thirty-two people are thinking deeply and furiously. Minds are going to war with every neuron at their disposal.

Liu moved her queen pawn, and I responded with a slightly obscure variation of the Grunfeld Defense, as my father had suggested. Soon my king was safely castled behind my bishop in a wall-like pawn formation called a fianchetto, and we were moving into the middle game on fairly even terms.

This was one of the stronger games I had ever played. Liu

had seen my low rating and was clearly surprised—she wrinkled her nose in frustration and dug her fists into her cheeks, and her black eyes never glanced up from the board. She may have been reading a novel when I walked up, but she was concentrating fiercely on chess now.

You don't have to stay at your board during a tournament. You can get up and walk around, provided that you don't give or get advice from anyone. Forty minutes into my game with Liu, I lost a pawn. It didn't mean that the game was over, but she now had a significant advantage, and she was pressing it mercilessly.

I made a move, stood up, stretched, and headed out for a bathroom break and to regroup. I was sluicing some cold water on my face when I heard two players talking near me. "Did you see what happened on board three?"

"No, what?"

"This grandmaster no one's ever heard of is self-destructing. He just dropped his rook."

"You're kidding? Talk about choking early."

"The rumor is that he's some kind of a wacko. Who ever heard of a grandmaster dropping a rook in round one?"

I hurried out and saw that a little crowd had collected on the dais, around my father's table. I walked up and stood behind him so that I wouldn't distract him. Dad was sitting with his arms folded tightly, a look of intense ferocity on his face. He wasn't moving even a muscle, but I could tell how tense he was. He looked like the slightest sound or movement might pulverize him.

I stepped closer so I could see the pieces. He was indeed a rook down. It was a complex position, but his opponent, Marciano—a rail-thin college-age supernerd wearing a *Star Trek* T-shirt—looked supremely confident. This was his chance to beat a grandmaster and he was going for it. As I watched, he lifted his queen and slammed it down so hard the table shook. When a supernerd attacks, it can be frightening.

My father didn't hesitate. He slammed down a knight even more furiously in counterattack. "Check," he said.

The supernerd shrugged and took Dad's knight. Now my father was a rook and a knight down.

A shocked whisper went up from the small crowd watching the game. I saw George Liszt stand up from board two and walk over to take a look.

"Check," my father announced again, this time moving a bishop far across its diagonal.

The expert took a little longer this time.

George Liszt smiled and sat back down at his game.

I felt someone walk up next to me and saw that it was Liu. I was surprised to see her there—her concentration on our own game had been total. But now she was watching my father play, and she threw a quick and curious glance at me, too.

Dad made two more rapid moves, and suddenly the geeky expert saw the trap he had fallen into. He might be up a rook and a knight, but he was about to get force mated and even I could see that there was no way out. He might get checkmated in two moves, or he could prolong it to five or six, but it was coming. He looked up at the ceiling, back at the chessboard, muttered something that sounded like a Klingon curse, and exhaled a long breath. Then he reached out and flicked over his king. "Awesome game, man."

My father shook his hand.

There was a rustle on the dais. I realized that the small crowd was applauding. "Quiet, quiet," a tournament official scolded. *"You must be silent."*

The applause quickly faded as the crowd began to break up, but not before George Liszt's voice called out two words from table number two, in a tone straight from a horror movie: *"Heeeee's baaaaccckkkkk!"*

I returned to my board and sat down, and Liu sat facing me. I fought hard for another thirty minutes, but she was just too strong. Our chess coach didn't like us to ever resign. "Don't give up," he always said. "Your opponent can make a mistake up to the very last move. Sit and get checkmated." But after more than an hour of tough chess, I knocked over my king. "Good game," I whispered.

"Really good," she admitted. "For a pushover, you played one hell of a game."

We reported our result to the scorer's table, and then we walked out the gaping doors into the ballroom lobby. "My mom's still playing," Liu said. "I saw her when we walked by."

"My dad's probably up in our room," I replied. "Decompressing from that first game."

"Who could blame him, after that?" she asked. "A rook sacrifice, and the forced mate was gorgeous. He really hasn't played in thirty years?"

"Nope," I told her. "I should probably go check on him. Nice meeting you, Liu. Good luck the rest of the way." I held out my hand.

She looked back at me and took my hand. "Good luck to you." Her hand still felt small and warm, and this time when we shook she gave me a little squeeze. "Can I ask you one question? You really don't know why your father gave up chess?"

"I don't have a clue," I told her. "Whatever happened, he doesn't want to talk about it. He did tell me one possible reason, but I don't think he was being serious."

"What did he say?" she asked.

I looked into Liu's glittering black eyes. "That he quit because he realized that playing in chess tournaments was a really bad way of trying to meet a nice girl."

She stuck out her tongue at me, and I turned away and headed for the elevators.

11

I let myself into our suite and heard the lowing. It was a low mooing chant that repeated itself over and over, and even though there were no words I could tell it was my father's voice. It was coming from his bedroom. "Dad?"

The lowing stopped. "Daniel? Is that you?"

"Are you okay?" I asked.

"Fine. Come in."

I walked into his bedroom. My father was lying on the rug on his back. He was wearing one of the hotel's white terry cloth robes and he had a white towel over his eyes.

"What was that sound?" I asked. "It sounded like someone was strangling a cow in here."

"That was a deep breathing exercise. It helps relieve tension and stabilize the heart rate. How did your game go?"

"Lost it," I told him. "She was really strong. But I think I played well. What's the matter with your heart?"

"Nothing. I just checked my blood pressure and it's barely elevated. But when I play chess I can't stop myself from getting tense." He removed the towel from his eyes and looked up at me. "Did you save the score sheet from your game?"

I dug it out of my pocket. When you play a tournament game, you have to record all the moves using an algebraic shorthand, which they taught us in chess club. That way, if a disagreement breaks out about a position, the tournament referee can use the score sheets to settle the matter. Also, if you write your moves down, you can replay the game later and analyze it. "When you're done relaxing, I'll set up the pieces and let's play it through," I suggested.

"Hand it over."

I gave him the score sheet, and he read it while lying flat on his back, his eyes flicking down the column of moves. "Good start," he muttered. "Here's where you went wrong. You should have challenged her for control of the center. Whoever controls the center of the battlefield makes his opponent fight on the wings."

"Can you really play the whole game out in your head?" I asked, amazed.

"What's so hard about visualizing a chessboard? There are only sixty-four squares." He finished scanning the sheet and handed it back. "Not bad, Daniel. I'm impressed. Next time you drop a pawn in the middle game, counterattack. When you're playing a good player and they get an advantage, you have to shake things up. Otherwise they'll just trade pieces and grind you down."

"I saw the end of your game," I told him. "Two guys were talking about you in the bathroom. They thought you had blundered away your rook. They didn't realize it was a brilliant sacrifice."

"I don't know about brilliant, but it got the job done." He studied my face for a moment and then he asked, "What else did they say about me?"

"Nothing." I looked down at the plush carpeting.

"Come on," he said. "Out with it."

I met his eyes. "One of them said he'd heard that you were a wacko grandmaster from long ago."

"Wacko, huh?" Dad sat up.

"They were just a couple of fools gossiping in a bathroom. Anyway, you showed them a flash of genius."

"'Genius,'" he repeated softly. "'Brilliant.' Daniel, these are lovely words you're coming up with lately . . . that you haven't attributed to your father before."

"Well, I never saw you play chess before," I pointed out, my voice practically glowing with pride and excitement. "You really played like a grandmaster! That supernerd expert was going right for your jugular. He thought he had you cooked. And all the time you were waiting to spring your devious trap. It was just . . . so cool to watch."

Dad stood up and nodded, looking grateful but also oddly sad. "Strange—I guess I never realized how important it was for you to see me do really well at something."

"I did feel very proud," I told him. "Is that a bad thing? I mean, I know you're a good accountant, but I can't really watch you do that."

"I'm a better than average accountant," he said. "But I was a *very* good chess player, for a wacko." He said it with a smile, but then he broke off for a moment, deep in thought. "Daniel . . ." I could see that he was tempted to tell me his deep, dark secret—why he had given up the game he loved thirty years ago. I didn't want to pry, but I was very curious to hear the real reason. Then he flinched and I saw him pull back, as if he had realized it would be too painful to talk about. "I'm going to take a shower," he said. "Dr. Sam was stuck in what looked like a marathon game, so Randolph moved our dinner reservation back. We have about an hour to kill. You might want to check out the pool."

"Isn't it a little late for a swim?" I asked.

"Apparently not," Dad said. "A friend of yours called a few minutes ago. She said she was heading down to the pool. She invited you to join her."

"Liu?" I asked, maybe a little too eagerly.

"No," Dad said, "I believe her name was Britney." He shot me a grin. "For a young man who claims to have trouble with girls, you seem to have your share of female admirers."

"You got that wrong," I told him. "Britney is Brad Kinney's girlfriend. She also happens to be the prettiest girl in our school. Believe me, the only thing she feels for me is pity."

"I wouldn't be so sure of that, kiddo," Dad said, heading into the bathroom. He turned on the shower, but his voice floated out above the sound of running water: "You ignore the insight of Grandmaster Pratzer at your peril."

12

The Palace Royale pool was located next to the hotel gym, on the third floor. I pushed through the doors, wearing my bathing suit and a T-shirt, and saw that the pool was almost deserted. A family was in the shallow end—the parents playing with their two tots, who were equipped with balloonlike flotation devices on arms and legs. In the deep end, a shark swam back and forth from one side to the other, knifing through the water so quickly it left a boiling silvery wake.

Of course it wasn't really a shark. It was the top swimmer at the Loon Lake Academy, Brad Kinney, getting his laps in before dinner. Perched on a lounge chair on the deep side of the pool, wearing a teensy-weensy purple bikini and watching him swim, was Britney. She was holding a stopwatch, and her eyes never left Brad as he did a flip turn and set off at turbo speed for the other side.

I walked over to her and tried not to stare. I'm pretty sure no one has ever looked that good in a purple bikini in the history of the world. "Hey, Britney."

Her eyes left the swimming champion and focused on me. "Hi, Daniel. How did your first game go?"

"I lost," I told her. "But it doesn't matter. The rest of the team will pick up the slack."

"You'll win the next one," she said. And then she added, "Your dad sounds nice. Thanks for coming down. When Brad swims his laps I have no one to talk to."

In the water beneath us, Brad flashed by and was gone. "How many does he do?" I asked.

"A hundred," she said. "And he never slows down. Isn't that amazing?"

"Remarkable," I agreed. "So what are you doing in Manhattan on a Friday night?"

"We were going to come tomorrow, but my mom got invited to some kind of charity ball this evening. I have to go with her, so I won't be able to come to the steak house. But we can all go out to dinner tomorrow."

"Sounds like a plan," I said. "Well, maybe I should jump in the shallow end and move my arms a little and pretend I can swim."

She laughed. "Come on. I'm sure you can swim just fine."

"Not like that," I said, as Brad motored by.

"No one swims like that," Britney responded softly.

"I'm off to do my dog paddle. Catch you later," I told her. "Have a ball at the charity ball. Looking forward to meeting your mom."

"Thanks. She's eager to hang out with the team—" Britney broke off, and I was surprised to see tension in her face. "I don't know exactly how she'll fit in," she admitted, sounding a little worried.

"What's the matter?" I asked.

"Nothing," she said quickly. She hesitated and then added: "My mom's been through a rough time, and she's a bit of a character, but I guess all parents are, right?"

"Absolutely," I assured her. "My dad is short, bald, and the poorest father at Loon Lake. Believe me, if I can bring him on this trip, you shouldn't have any worries about your mom."

Britney flashed a grateful smile. "You don't take yourself too seriously. That's kind of a rare thing at our school."

"If I took myself too seriously, I'd be disappointed," I told her with a grin. "But seriously, if your mom raised you, I'm sure she must be pretty cool."

"She is," Britney agreed in a low voice. "Thank you . . ."

"What are you two whispering about?" a voice demanded.

I whirled around to see that Brad had finished his hundred laps, climbed out of the pool, and was toweling off just a few feet from us.

"Nothing," I said. "I was just wondering how you can swim so many laps without slowing down."

"This was nothing," Brad told me, as if his usual workouts were twice as hard. Then he turned to Britney. "Did you get my time, baby?"

She looked down at the stopwatch. It was still running. She clicked it off. "I'm so sorry," she said. "I got distracted . . ."

"Yeah, well, I'm sorry, too," Brad growled. "Without a time, it's useless. I just wasted half an hour of training."

"You were really swimming fast," I told him.

Brad glared at me. "Did anybody invite you to speak?"

"No," I admitted.

"Then make yourself scarce, Patzer-face." He turned back to Britney. "I'm going to swim twenty laps of backstroke. Make sure you clock it to the second."

13

"So you're a bean counter, Morris?" Randolph Kinney said, taking a gulp from his gin martini and wrapping his tongue around an olive like an octopus seizing a small fish with its tentacle. Everyone but me had won, so the Mind Cripplers had posted five points in the first round and our host was in a genial mood. "What firm are you at?"

"Just a small outfit in Jersey," my father replied, taking a sip from his glass of tomato juice.

We were standing at the bar of the Patagonia Steakhouse in a fashionable downtown section of Manhattan called Tribeca. The lighting was dim, the portions looked huge, and the high-ceilinged space was packed with diners even though it was past nine. Eric and Brad were chatting on cell phones, drawing dirty looks from other patrons at the bar. From what I overheard, Eric was browbeating his lab partner about a big project due next week, while Brad was making plans with Britney for Saturday night.

I was standing next to my dad, sipping a ginger ale and wondering if I should jump into the adult conversation and try to rescue him. "So what's the name of your small firm?" Randolph pressed. "I do lots of work with bean counters in Jersey. I'm sure I've heard of you guys."

"Haug and Gilooly," my father said.

"Haug and Gilooly," Randolph repeated, making the names sound even sillier than normal. "Never heard of it. Must be *really* small."

"Sounds like Howdy Doody," Dr. Chisolm contributed, well into his second large glass of red wine. "But all those bean counters have silly names."

My father smiled at him. "So you're a sawbones?"

Dr. Chisolm's eyes narrowed. I don't think anyone had referred to him as a sawbones in a while. "I'm Chief of Cardiac Surgery at Hackensack Hospital."

"I'm kind of surprised to see you at a steak house," Dad said. "You must know more about cholesterol than any of us. Doesn't slicing into a rare steak make you think of the operating table?"

"I did become a vegetarian for a while during my residency," Dr. Chisolm admitted. "But I can handle it now. You just have to learn to separate."

Dad turned to Mr. Kinney. "And you're a hedge trimmer?"

"You made that up," Mr. Kinney said. "That's pretty good. But, yeah, I run a four-billion-dollar global macro hedge fund that tilts toward technology . . ."

Meanwhile, I heard Brad telling Britney: "The steak house looks okay. Nothing special."

A hostess walked over to us and said, "Kinney party? Your table is ready."

"Gotta go chow down," Brad grunted into the phone. "If I were you, I'd drag your mom out of there before she gets going. And watch out for those New York prep boys." He hung up.

"Make sure you triple-check those graphs," Eric ordered his lab partner, and then he also punched out.

"This way, please," the hostess said, and we followed her through the restaurant to a table for six, in its own private alcove. I sat between my father and Eric. My family didn't go out to eat often, and when we did it was usually for pizza or Chinese, or on special occasions to a nice family chain restaurant. Patagonia was by far the most elegant restaurant I'd ever been in.

"Welcome. I'm Claudio, your server," a tall young man with an earring said. "Let me tell you about today's specials. We have . . ."

"Save it," Randolph cut him off. "We already know what we want. I'll have the bone-in rib eye, bloody. Put something green next to it. And we need some wine." He glanced at Dr. Chisolm, who was almost finished with his second glass. "Sam, what is that piss you're drinking?"

"It's an estate-bottled Malbec," Dr. Chisolm said.

"Malbec went to hell in '76 when frost killed off the old vines in Bordeaux," Mr. Kinney declared.

"Actually, we have more than two dozen Argentine Malbecs on our list, several of which are stunning," Claudio interjected proudly.

"Actually, they're not," Mr. Kinney told him, running his eyes down the extensive wine list. "So let's not waste time. Bring us this Rhone—and let's pair it with this Barolo. Now, I'm hungry, so let's get some food on the table, pronto."

"Yes, sir," Claudio said, swallowing his pride and no doubt imagining his tip.

The rest of us ordered, and we were soon tucking into steaks the size of manhole covers. I hadn't realized how hungry I was. Chess tournaments are very hard work. The game against Liu had exhausted me. I read somewhere that a grandmaster can lose between six to eight pounds of body weight during an average game just by concentrating so hard. Maybe this tournament would help Dad lose a little of his potbelly.

He had barely touched his steak, and he was understandably staying out of a conversation, between the two other dads, on who drove the better sports coupe. Meanwhile, Eric and Brad were going through the girls at our school year by year, picking out the cutest ones and rating them on a scale of one to ten.

I kept quiet and ate and thought we might get through this dinner without a major blowup.

Then the table conversations changed. Eric and Brad began planning what they were going to do with their share of the first-place prize money. Meanwhile, their fathers shifted from sports cars to the importance of winning. There was a candle on our table, and Brad's father held his index finger above the flame. "It's all in the mind," he said, slowly lowering his finger till the flame licked his skin. I swear I could smell flesh burning. His eyes were fixed and hard.

My father reached out and pulled Mr. Kinney's hand away from the candle. "You don't have to do that," he said. "We already know you're tough."

"It's not about being tough," Randolph told him. "It's a lesson I want the boys to take away from this weekend. If you want to win, you've got to be willing to take risks and endure things that others can't."

As if on cue Dr. Chisolm got up from his chair and bent over all the way to the floor and then walked his feet up the wall of our dining alcove so that he was standing on his hands. He kicked away from the wall and began walking on his hands. Finally, with a great effort, he slowly picked his left hand up and stood on just his right, his face turning red from the pressure of his full body weight. "I used to be able to hold this position for two minutes," he grunted, putting his other hand back down and then falling to his knees.

"Still pretty studly, Dad," Eric said proudly. And then he told all of us: "Dad was a varsity gymnast at Stanford. He tried out for the Olympic team."

"What about you, Morris?" Randolph asked. "Got anything you want to show the boys?"

Dad thought about it and smiled. "I've got one or two things up my sleeve," he said. "Check this out."

I knew what was coming and almost couldn't bear to watch. He thrust his head slightly forward on his neck like a turtle poking out of its shell, tilted his chin up so that his bald pate gleamed under the one ceiling light, and concentrated.

"What the hell's he doing?" Eric asked. "Is he trying to levitate?"

"No, he's wiggling his ear," Brad snorted.

"Both ears," Dad said proudly. "And watch this." He took off his glasses, and one of his eyebrows cocked up while the other one arched downward. "Pretty nifty, huh?"

"Morris, as one Mind Crippler to another, you need some new material," Randolph Kinney told him, and the four of them burst into laughter.

I found myself on my feet, speaking a little too loudly. "My father's the only grandmaster at this table, and he just won today with a brilliant rook sacrifice, so maybe all of you should shut your mouths."

They stopped laughing. "Looks like Patzer-face is ready to take us all on," Brad said with a grin.

"Yeah, well we probably shouldn't laugh at a team member," Eric said. "Even an ear-wiggling one."

"We weren't laughing at you, Morry," Randolph chimed in. "Is it okay if I call you that? And I did hear about that rook sacrifice today. I'd love to see the game. But now that we've had a couple of glasses of wine I've gotta ask you something." He lowered a glass of expensive Rhone wine and said: "Why on earth did you give up chess for the last thirty years?"

The table suddenly quieted.

"Personal reasons," my father said, looking straight ahead.

"What possible personal reason could there be for giving up what you're best at?" Dr. Chisolm followed up, his cheeks red. He had drunk too much too quickly, and it seemed to bring out the aggressive, nasty side of his character. "No offense, but you work for Howdy Doody, and you wiggle your ears and move your eyes like Mr. Potato Head . . ."

Eric and Brad howled with laughter.

"But you were a monster at chess," the heart surgeon admitted. "I googled you and some of your games won brilliancy prizes and are posted online with grandmaster commentary. I played through a couple and they're amazing. And I saw that you came in second at the U.S. Open one year—back when you were still a teenager. So what possible personal reason could make you quit . . . ?"

I glanced at my father. It was news to me that he had finished second in a U.S. Open.

Dad stood up. "Daniel, I've finished my steak and I think we should go," he said with quiet dignity. I stood up next to him, without a word.

"Don't storm off, Morry," Mr. Kinney said. "We didn't mean anything. Sit back down. We were just naturally curious about why you gave up something you were so good at. Stay and have dessert. They make a mean cheesecake, and I was going to order a special port."

"I don't need your special port," my father told him, looking him in the eye. "Thanks for dinner. Come on, Daniel."

We started to walk away.

"Morry," Randolph Kinney called again, louder. "We apologize if we offended you. You don't want the lesson you teach your son to be to walk away from his own team, do you?"

Dad whirled around. "Let's get this out in the open. The only reason you invited Daniel to be on this team was so that I would help you guys win. But what's even worse is that your two sons have made my boy feel like crud since the moment we showed up." My father's eyes swung to Dr. Chisolm. "And just so you know—one reason I quit chess was that I couldn't control my temper, and that included nearly killing a rude asshole with my bare hands."

Dad said this softly, his face deadpan, but for a moment his eyes flashed with such a maniacal gleam that Dr. Chisolm cringed.

"Let's go, Daniel," my dad said.

We headed away from the table. "Morry, come back," Randolph called after us, and there was a note of pleading in his voice. Suddenly he barked out what sounded like a military order. *"Get back here now, Morris.* I've spent significant money putting this team together. Damn it, nobody walks out on me."

But we left the Patagonia Steakhouse without a backward glance and the cool outside air felt good. "I think you scared the pants off Dr. Chisolm," I told my father.

"He's a piece of work," Dad said. "I feel a little sorry for his son."

"You put him in his place. You did great. Except for wiggling your ears."

Dad took my arm as we crossed a street. "Okay, son. I'll get some new material. Want to walk back? It's a couple of miles."

"Lead on," I said. "The night is still young."

14

We headed uptown on an avenue that was mostly empty, except for the steady stream of cars. Their lights swept the sidewalks and lit up the apartment lobbies where doormen stood as still as statues. Every now and then we would pass a bar or a restaurant, and knots of people would emerge, hail taxis, and disappear.

"I shouldn't have said what I said," Dad muttered. "It must have sounded like I was threatening Chisolm."

"He provoked you," I told him. "He called you Mr. Potato Head. I think he was drunk."

"Still," he said. He stuck his hands in his pockets and walked half a block in silence. He finally took a deep breath and said, "Daniel, I want you to hear this from me."

"You really don't owe me any kind of explanation. You're doing this for me. That's enough."

"It's not enough," he said. "I lied to my son about who I

really am. And the hell of it is that you've never seen me really good at anything before . . ."

"You're good at plenty of things," I protested. "Anyway, what does it matter?"

He waved me into silence. "It matters. Every son wants his father to shine at something. Chisolm's right, you've got to be wondering why I gave up the thing I was best at . . . and in many ways loved the most." We reached an intersection and waited for the light to change. When it flashed green, he took my arm and we headed across. "You're going to hear it anyway, from George Liszt or some gossip in a bathroom who doesn't know the real story. I'd prefer you hear my version first."

"Okay," I said, trying to keep from sounding too curious. "What's the real story of Grandmaster Pratzer?"

We walked side by side, our feet rising and falling together. "Do you know who Bobby Fischer and Paul Morphy were?"

"Fischer, sure. He was a great chess player. Some say the greatest who ever lived. He won the world championship back in the eighties."

"The seventies," Dad corrected me. "He obliterated three top grandmasters to get to face Boris Spassky, the world champion. Then he destroyed Spassky to take away the title from the Russians. It was a great Cold War victory, and an incredible chess feat, given how much the Russians valued chess and worked together to try to stop him. Do you know what happened to Fischer after that?"

"He cracked up," I said. "And I read that he died a little while ago."

"Cracked up is a kind word for it. He became a recluse. Grew bitter. Paranoid. Irrational. Turned his back on all his friends, his country, and the chess world that had created his celebrity. He made anti-American comments, anti-Semitic comments—he said that he was glad that 9/11 happened. He served months in a Japanese jail. He died alone, despised, and ridiculed. You couldn't find a more miserable end to such a promising life." Dad was quiet for a few seconds and then whispered, "Unless you look at Paul Morphy."

"I've heard the name," I said. "But all I know is he was an early chess player."

"Morphy was the greatest," my father told me softly. "Even Fischer acknowledged that. Morphy was from a leading New Orleans family, back in the nineteenth century. His uncle was one of the strongest players in America, nicknamed the 'Chess King of New Orleans,' but by the time Morphy was twelve he could beat his uncle blindfolded. He lived and played before the great advances in modern chess theory, but if he'd been able to study them, he would have destroyed anyone around today. It wouldn't have even been close."

There was a peculiar tone in my father's voice—both hero worship and a kind of closeness or kinship. I guessed that Dad had spent a lot of time playing through Morphy's games and thinking about the man's life. "He went to Europe to play the strongest players of his day and test himself. He destroyed all of them, except Staunton, who refused to play him. Everyone acknowledged Morphy as the most brilliant world champion the world had ever seen. If you play through his games, their clarity of thought and inventiveness is breathtaking. It's like . . . listening to Mozart."

"What happened to him?" I asked.

"He wanted to be a lawyer. He had an incredible memory so he memorized the entire Louisiana legal code. But then he started spending more and more time by himself, in his parents' house. He became a recluse. Gave way to depression and extreme paranoia. Lost all his friends. Never had a career. Never got married or had kids. He stayed in his room. He would only eat the food his mother cooked him. He died of brain congestion after going for a walk in midday heat and then climbing into a cold bath, a famous, lonely eccentric . . . or you could call him a depressed and paranoid wacko."

I looked back at him. "Just like Fischer."

"Peas in a pod." Dad nodded. "The two great giants of American chess, with the two saddest and loneliest ends you could script for them."

"You think it was the chess?" I asked.

"Who knows why they both melted down," my father said. "Psychologists would say they were predisposed to it, that both men had underlying conditions. I'm sure that's true. But, Daniel, chess on that level can take you to a very dark place. The level of concentration and aggression you need to bring to bear is frightening. Some people can handle it, and others can't."

I sensed he was done with Fischer and Morphy, and was now talking about Pratzer. "And you couldn't?" I asked.

Suddenly there was a tremendous peal of thunder. Lightning flashed, and the skies opened up with a torrent of cold rain. We ran for it up the avenue and were soon soaked to our skin. There were no taxis, and no places to take shelter. "There," Dad said and pointed.

A sign for a tavern flashed at the next corner. It was a bar called the Clover Leaf, and we hurried in through the heavy wooden door. There was a basketball game on the TV, and a dozen or so men and two women sipping drinks at the bar. We found a booth and looked at each other and laughed as water dripped off us onto the table.

I went into the bathroom and wiped myself down with a paper towel, and when I came back my dad was sitting with his elbows on the old wooden table. He had ordered two drinks— a ginger ale for me and a whiskey for himself. He almost never drank alcohol, but I saw him take a sip of the whiskey and it seemed to warm and relax him. "You okay?" he asked.

"That was some rain. I thought we might drown."

"We were lucky to find this place," Dad said. And then he set his whiskey down and picked up the story right where he had left off. "I told you about Fischer and Morphy. Not that I would ever put myself in their company, but you might as well hear about me."

He leaned slightly forward and lowered his voice. "There was an attic room in my parents' house in Hoboken where I used to study chess when everyone had gone to bed. It was very quiet. One small window. A bare overhead lightbulb. Sometimes I spent whole nights there, and then showered and went to school. I replayed the games of the old masters and climbed into Capablanca's mind, and went to war side by side with Morphy. I was a lonely kid with no friends. That became my real life. And I loved it for a while. But it was taking me to a dangerous and solitary place."

He broke off, took a sip of his whiskey, and then finished his tale. "It further isolated me. It unhinged me, and destabilized me. My whole source of pride and self-esteem became chess. I absolutely had to win, to go to war and kill, so badly that . . . the worst parts of me were taking over . . . and I couldn't control it. Everyone was telling me how great I was, and I was starting to travel to international matches . . . and deep down . . . I was afraid of what was happening. I could feel myself unraveling . . ."

"So you quit to save yourself?" I asked.

"There were some incidents," he admitted. "One in particular . . . that was really bad. I ended up being hospitalized and on medication. When I got out, I quit chess. Cold turkey. The doctors didn't tell me to do it—I did it myself. I cut the head off the beast. I was never good at sports, but I started speed-walking, and I tried to take better care of my health. I forced myself to come out of my shell, and I finally made a friend or two. I went off to college and majored in business, and met your mother, and I never told her about chess. My parents understood some of what I had gone through and respected my decision to quit, and they never talked about it either."

"Okay," I said, "I understand now. I think you made a wise choice."

"I've wondered over the years," he admitted. "I was very strong, Daniel. I could have been a serious chess player. Maybe not a Fischer or a Morphy, but one of the top players of my generation. Instead, I went into a career where things are very steady and there aren't major surprises. Everybody jokes about accountants being boring, but steady sounded good to me. Plus it pays the bills, and I get to work with people I like. So I never went to that dark place again. Instead I have a wife and a family, and a relatively happy home." He managed a smile.

I smiled back at him. "It *is* a happy home. Except for my nutty sister."

"Paul Morphy and Bobby Fischer never experienced that kind of happiness," he said. "I'll take what I've got . . ." And his voice trailed off. He turned away, and I saw that he was trembling. I got up and went over to his side of the booth, and I'm not sure how it happened but I kind of put my arms around him and he hugged me back.

"Sorry I haven't been a father you could be more proud of," he whispered. "Someone more involved in your life. One effect of what I went through—I know I'm a little distant, and self-absorbed in my work. It helps me stay on an even keel, but I'm aware of it and I feel bad about it. It's not because I don't love you."

"This is starting to sound like a soap opera," I told him. "And I'm really sorry I made you come here and dig this all up again. Anytime you want to quit and go back home, just say the word."

The bartender strolled over with a slightly concerned look and asked, "Everything okay here, gentlemen?"

We released each other and sat there a little awkwardly. "Fine," Dad said. "We're just having a father-son moment. We'll take the check."

"Coming right up," the bartender told us, and walked away.

"I'm sure I can handle it for two more days," Dad said. "But it does amaze me after all these years how the darkness starts to take hold of me again. Anyway, now you know, Daniel. We should get back to the hotel. I'll spring for a cab. Tomorrow's first round starts at nine."

He paid the check and we left the bar and waited on the curb for a taxi with its light on. "Thanks for telling me what happened," I said. "But for what it's worth, I bet Paul Morphy would have been proud of the way you played today."

Grandmaster Pratzer smiled and gave me a wink and then hailed a cab.

15

The phone rang in our suite at exactly eight-thirty to the second. I knew before I answered it that it was Randolph Kinney, punctual as always. My father came out of his bedroom and I held my hand over the receiver and pointed next door. "Team meeting," I said softly. "Do we go?"

I had slept well after our steak dinner and long stroll through lower Manhattan, but I was pretty sure he hadn't slept a wink. I had been dimly aware of him pacing around during the night, and he had deep circles under his eyes that made him look a little like a hooded owl. "We go," he said. "But on our own terms."

"We'll be there in a few minutes," I told Mr. Kinney. "We've got some stuff to do first." I hung up.

Ten minutes later we knocked on the door, and the hedge fund titan himself greeted us. He looked impatient, but he was clearly trying to mend fences. "How are you, Daniel?" he asked.

"Morris, come on in." We hadn't gotten more than ten feet inside the door when he said: "Pratzers, we want to extend a sincere apology for what happened last night, put it behind us, and make a fresh start. And this doesn't just come from me. It comes from all of us."

Dr. Chisolm stepped forward. "I had a little too much to drink last night and said some things I shouldn't have. Morris, will you shake my hand?" He held out his right hand, and for a long moment it dangled in empty air.

My father took it and they shook. "I said a few things I shouldn't have, too," Dad admitted. "And I'm not planning to wiggle my ears in public again anytime soon."

Dr. Chisolm gave an appreciative chuckle and Mr. Kinney threw a look at Brad and Eric. They both stepped toward me. "Hey, bro," Brad said, and it seemed strange to hear him calling me anything but Patzer-face. "I'm glad you're on this team and . . . sorry for being such a hard-ass."

"We think you can make a real contribution," Eric added, and then his voice trailed off as if he couldn't quite figure out exactly how or to what.

They held out their hands, and—feeling a little foolish—I shook them.

"I'd like to further atone for any lingering hard feelings by inviting everyone to Chez André tonight," Mr. Kinney announced magnanimously. "It's one of the finest French restaurants in this whole damn city. Let's have a great second day of chess and then a haute cuisine feast. It's all on me. What do you say?"

"Thanks, but I'm not sure I'm ready for another big dinner," my father told him.

"No pressure. Think it over," Randolph said. "It's the least I can do. And now that we've put that behind us . . . let's talk about today. We have our work cut out for us," he noted, looking just a little worried.

"They posted the next round pairings," Eric explained. "Mr. Pratzer, you're playing a tough master named Voorhees. We know him from Jersey tournaments, and he's a shark. Daniel, you've got an unrated named Lowery. The rest of us all drew opponents rated higher than we are."

"To hell with ratings," Mr. Kinney muttered. "We just have to play smart."

"I agree," my dad told him. "Ratings are overrated."

"There you go!" Mr. Kinney said, clapping his hands. "I want five points out of this next round." He glanced at his watch. "Now, if everyone's agreeable, I'll deliver the team prayer. One knee, gentlemen."

Silly as it was, we all got down.

"Moment of silence," Randolph commanded, and we were quiet. I saw my dad bring his arms together and thought for a moment that he might be clasping his hands to pray. Then I saw that the fingers of his right hand were on his left wrist, and I realized that he was taking his pulse.

"Let us pray," the hedge fund king said. "Lord, watch over

the Mind Cripplers and keep us tight—" Before he got through any more of the prayer, a loud and insistent tapping sounded on the door.

"Who could that be?" Mr. Kinney asked, annoyed.

A female voice called out: "Boys? Helloooo? Are you up and decent yet?"

"It's *her*," he muttered, throwing a look at Brad.

"Don't blame me," Brad said.

"Let's try to finish the team prayer," Dr. Chisolm suggested.

Mr. Kinney picked up where he had left off. "Lord, keep us tight and keep our eyes on the prize and—"

"*Yooo-hooo, booooysssss?* We have snacks, so open up," the voice called again.

Mr. Kinney broke off. "Aw, to hell with it," he muttered, got to his feet, and walked to the door. He opened it and said, "Mariel, what a delightful surprise."

A very attractive blond woman in a pink jogging outfit stepped into the room. Her hair was coiffed, her nails were manicured, and her teeth were so white that when she smiled it was almost blinding. It was Britney's mom, I figured. She looked around at us, and her eyes settled on Dr. Chisolm. "We needed you last night, Sam. Some old geezer blew a gasket and dropped dead at the charity ball."

"I'm glad I missed that . . ." he started to say.

She talked through him. "Brad, did you get your laps in this morning? There's a meet coming up and we're counting on you to break the school record again." Her blue eyes flicked to Eric. "Speaking of achievements, did I hear something about senior class speaker that I wasn't supposed to? Congratulations, even though it's still hush-hush. And you must be Daniel."

I blinked and tried not to stare at her teeth. "Yes, ma'am." I glimpsed Britney walking in behind her, trying to guide a room service waiter who was carrying a tray containing enough doughnuts for a college football team and also a giant thermos of hot coffee.

"Britney said you were polite. Please call me Mariel. And you must be Daniel's father. I've never met a grandmaster before. I'm fascinated by how your mind works."

"It will work better with some hot coffee," Dad told her, stepping over to help the waiter with the thermos.

Mariel found a reason to touch each one of us in turn—to fix Dr. Chisolm's collar and pat Brad's shoulder and brush some lint off my dad's sweater.

"Well now," she said. "This is all so exciting. Our team is in first place. And I heard about Chez André tonight."

Mr. Kinney reluctantly muttered: "I hope you and Britney can join us."

"We wouldn't miss it. Doughnuts, boys, time to get your sugar fix. Who wants coconut?" She practically crammed one into Randolph's mouth. "What about you, Grandmaster?"

"I'm watching my weight," Dad said. "I'll stick with the coffee."

"One doughnut never hurt a waistline," she told him. "Here, double cream is my favorite."

"Mom, he said he doesn't want one," Britney whispered sharply. "And we can't just invite ourselves to dinner . . ."

Mariel glanced at her daughter, and for just a moment her confidence seemed to slip and she looked noticeably insecure. She immediately covered it by starting to talk fast again. "You should have a doughnut yourself, honey. You're all skin and bones. How about cinnamon?" Suddenly the alarm on her cell phone went off. "Spa time," she announced. "Come on, Brit, there's nothing like a massage to start the day off right. We'll see you all later."

She headed out, and as she passed Mr. Kinney she bestowed a two-cheek European goodbye kiss on him that looked like it was intended to suck the skin off the front of his skull. "Bye, Randy. Good luck, team."

Britney followed her mother out, throwing a backward look at Brad, and for a moment at me, that was both angry and apologetic. Then the door closed and they were both gone.

"I think she's fond of you, Randolph," Dr. Chisolm noted with a wry smile. "And I hear she got five million and the house in the divorce."

"Good God," the hedge fund monarch said, wiping lipstick off his face. "Jesus, Brad."

"How is it my fault?" Brad wanted to know.

Randolph seemed tempted to offer his son an explanation,

but instead he glanced at his watch. "Gentlemen, it's chess time. All team schisms are healed, all distractions have been banished to the spa. This is day two—*the extremely crucial day two*. There are three rounds, and we need lots and lots of points. Let's go, Mind Cripplers—off to war!"

16

Lowery turned out to be even more of a patzer-face than I was. He was a big lug of a kid—seventeen years old and at least six foot three and two hundred pounds—so it was strange to see him look so frightened. "Is this your first tournament?" he asked while I was filling out my scorecard. "It's my first one and my last one. Some of these people are freaky smart. The guy I played in the first round was a youth president of Mensa. Chess is an okay game, but it's like a religion to some of these dudes. Know what I mean?"

He seemed so nervous I felt sorry for him. "They're not as smart as they let on. Just try to have fun," I advised him.

"You call this fun?" he asked. "Fun is paintball or bowling with my buds. Check out my hand." His right hand was shaking so badly that he was having trouble writing my name and rating down on his score sheet.

We sat there waiting for the command to start our clocks. "So . . . do you study openings?" Lowery whispered.

"A little," I admitted.

"Yeah, right, I'm sure just a little bit." He popped a Lifesaver into his mouth and cracked it with his teeth.

Suddenly I felt a hand tap me on the shoulder. "Hey, Jersey boy." It was Liu. She was wearing tight black pants and some kind of silky dark top, and her hair was loose and hung almost to her hips.

"Be right back," I told Lowery, and got up from the table. "Hey, Catwoman."

"Don't make fun of my outfit or I'll claw your nose off," she warned.

"I like it," I told her. "How was your evening?"

"Boring," she said. "My team ate dinner in the hotel restaurant so they could study chess and get a good night's sleep. What about you guys?"

"We went to Tribeca for a steak dinner."

"I'm on the wrong team," she said ruefully.

"Actually, it was a disaster," I told her. "The other fathers wanted to know why my dad gave up chess, and they got rude. We ended up storming out of the restaurant."

"Sounds like maybe you're on the wrong team, too." Liu hesitated a beat. "Maybe we should hang out together tonight. With your dad and my mom. If you're free . . . ?"

It was the first time a girl had ever asked me out, and I tried not to look too surprised or eager. "Sounds good to me. Our team is planning another fancy dinner, but I know my dad isn't eager to go."

"Then let's have some fun," she proposed. "I think I know just the right place . . ."

"Chess players, start your clocks," the tournament announcer said.

"Gentlemen, start your engines." Liu imitated his tone perfectly. Then she said, "Good luck, Daniel. Play like you did yesterday and you might actually win one."

"Good luck to you, Catwoman," I told her. She gave me a little snarl and I returned to my table smiling.

"She's hot," Lowery said as I sat down. "Did you meet her here?"

"She beat me in the first round," I told him.

"You're lucky," he said. "The youth president of Mensa who whipped my ass was a nerd with zits."

I was going to play one of the lesser-known variations my father had shown me, but something told me I wouldn't need to get fancy with Lowery. Instead I played the main line of the Giuoco Piano, and sure enough Lowery fell into the dreaded Fried Liver. "This is a trap," he whispered after six moves, "isn't it?"

Normally I never talk to opponents during a match, but since he'd asked I whispered back: "It is. It's called the Fried Liver."

He swallowed. "Why do they call it that?"

" 'Cause if you fall into it, you'll soon be as dead as a piece of fried liver," I told him.

"Great," he muttered. "Terrific."

"*Shhhh,*" the player to his right hissed, and Lowery nodded apologetically and then let out a long sigh. The tournament hall was cool but he had already broken into a sweat. He took his time and came up with a few defensive moves, but they were the wrong ones. The one thing you can't do when you play the black side of the Fried Liver is let your king get pinned in the middle of the board. I soon had bishops and knights bearing down on his king, and the more he tried to defend the worse it got.

As I sat there playing moves I had memorized, I realized the truth of what my father had told me. Springing an opening trap isn't really chess—I wasn't outthinking Lowery on the field of mental combat. I was just playing moves someone else had worked out and put in a book that I had read. And, as easy and fun as it was for me to destroy Lowery, I realized it was just as easy for the higher-ranked players I played to do this to me. Dad had a point: if I was to have any chance at doing well in this tournament, I would have to get my higher-rated opponents off the main lines and away from the openings they had memorized.

"Enough," Lowery said after twelve moves, and knocked over his king. "I'm tired of being a piece of fried meat. I'm out of here."

I shook his sweaty hand and handed in my score sheet and took a quick stroll around the hall, checking on other games. Liu was up a pawn to a serious-looking old gent with white hair, and bearing down on him. She was concentrating ferociously, but she felt my look and glanced up at me questioningly. I gave her a thumbs-up, and she flashed me a congratulatory smile before lowering her eyes to the board.

Eric was losing to a master and not looking happy about it. He played chess the way he did everything in life—grinding and fighting for every inch. The master he was playing was much higher rated and probably far more naturally gifted, but Eric was making him sweat blood for the point.

A few tables over I saw Brad, who was also engaged in a tough battle but managed to look cool and confident. While I was studying his board, I felt someone grab my arm. It was Grandmaster George Liszt. "Daniel? Come, I need to talk to you about your dad."

"No way," I said, and I tried to pull away, but the big man had the grip of a mountain gorilla.

"I think you'd better come," he rumbled. "He needs your help. The referee just warned him for talking to his opponent." I glanced toward the dais where the top players were playing. I could just make out my father, sitting bent over and concentrating intently. A wary tournament official hovered nearby. I took a step toward him, but Liszt held me back.

"He's okay for now," Liszt assured me, "but he'll flare up again soon, and then it'll be a slippery slope. I've seen this all before, and it wasn't pretty. The only way you'll have a chance of protecting your dad is if you know the truth. Are you brave enough to hear it?"

I looked up at him and allowed myself to be led away.

17

He led me out of the tournament ballroom, and we walked through the common area, past stands selling chess sets, books, and accessories. Liszt kept hold of my arm and chatted as if we were old friends out for a stroll. "My second round opponent crumbled like a piece of toast," he said, smirking. "Fifteen moves, and he was an expert, too. It happens to some strong players when they play grandmasters. They see my rating and they give up before they sit down at the board. I can see the fear in their eyes. And you won your game, right? This was your first blood?"

"Where are we going?" I asked. "What happened to my dad just now, and what else do you have to tell me?"

"This tournament isn't half bad," Liszt said. "Quite well run. As soon as he started running his mouth, the refs were right on it. He took the warning and shut up. I've always thought he knows that he's doing it, and that to a certain extent he can control it. But when he bottles it up, it gets much worse."

"What gets much worse?"

We were on a long escalator, descending toward the first floor lobby. "You look just like him, did you know that?" Liszt asked me. "The way he used to look."

"No, I don't . . ." I began to object.

"I've known him a lot longer than you have," he pointed out. "This way." He yanked me to one side, and we walked through the swinging glass doors of a coffee shop in the hotel's lobby. A corner table was open and in a minute I found myself sipping a cup of tea with milk and watching Grandmaster Liszt lick beads of chai latte off his mustache. "So," he said, "first of all, as you must have realized, I'm not exactly a pal of your father's."

"I gathered that."

"Nor would I say I am completely an enemy." He ran a hand through his shaggy beard. "I'm a very competitive guy and he was the best of us, and I never could quite accept that. I say, he *was* the best of us, because he's been away much too long. He's struggling now against Voorhees, and even if he wins this one he'll get thrashed by any of the top dozen players here. Ring rust. And he's not up on the latest theory." Liszt took another sip of latte and gave me a puzzled look. "What I don't get is that Morris made the right decision. He got out while he could. He left it behind before it destroyed him, and he made a clean break. I gather he has a career, and a family, completely outside of the chess world, and I haven't seen him at a tournament in thirty years. Why the hell did he come back?"

"I brought him back," I confessed. "Some kids from my

school were entering this tournament. They found out about him and asked me to get him on the team. He's doing this for me."

Liszt raised his bushy eyebrows, which looked like untended hedges, and nodded as if this was beginning to make sense. "Well, if you got him into this, you've got to get him out," the hulking grandmaster said. "And the sooner the better, or you may be guilty of patricide."

"Why?" I asked. "It's just one three-day tournament. I know he had some problems with his temper back in the day, but he says he can control it."

Liszt's deep rumble of laughter sounded like thunder in the mountains. "'Some problems with his temper'? That's rich." He jabbed a finger as thick as a banana in my direction. "Let me tell you a little about your dad's unfortunate difficulties controlling his temper. They almost killed him, not to mention poor Stanwick."

I looked back at him. There was still time to get up and walk out of this coffee shop and not listen to this. But I found myself asking: "Who is Stanwick?"

"Nelson Stanwick. I still see him in tournaments from time to time. He's just a shadow of what he was. The truth is I don't think he ever fully recovered."

I knew I was opening a door to something I didn't want to hear about, but I had to know. "Stop messing with my head," I told the big man. "Just tell me what happened."

"Sure," Liszt said, and I got the feeling he was enjoying

this. "Why not? That's why we're here. But first I'm going to get another latte. They charge so much and the cups are so small. You want something?"

I shook my head and watched him lumber to the counter. I knew I shouldn't be listening to my father's enemy tell tales about him. But at the same time, I was responsible for bringing him here, and I needed to know what the risks were. It seemed to me that a man who openly admitted that he didn't like my father could be depended on to tell me the full truth, ugly though it might be.

He sat back down with a second latte, and the chair groaned. "So," he said, "Morris Pratzer. I first saw him on the circuit back in the seventies. Bobby Fischer had won the title and American chess surged. The first big tournaments for kids with real prize money were held here in New York, at a hotel called the McAlpin. There were a dozen of us who were rising stars. Your dad came late to the table, but it didn't matter—the chess gods had given him something the rest of us didn't have."

"How good was he?" I asked. "He told me last night he never could have been a Fischer or a Morphy."

Liszt shrugged. "Probably Fischer and Morphy didn't think they could be Fischer or Morphy either. Who knows how good he could have been? In certain tournaments, in certain games, he played with a touch of genius. The rest of us were in awe . . . and jealous as hell."

"I hear he almost won a U.S. Open," I said.

"He was young but he dominated," the burly grandmaster said. "He won lots of tournaments, and he was beginning to be recognized internationally, but he was not a happy camper. I don't think I've ever seen such a lonely kid. He had no girl-friends. No pals. He didn't hang out with the rest of us. When he got to be about fifteen, and the tournament pressures mounted, it grew much worse. He would talk to himself. At first we thought maybe he was a schizophrenic, but it wasn't that. It was an outlet for him, a way to handle the pressure. I once roomed with him at an international in Madrid, and he kept me awake half the night with his gobbledygook. I finally told him to shut the hell up, and I was tempted to stuff a sock in his mouth. He didn't only talk to himself. He also talked to his opponents, the way he just did to Voorhees."

"Why didn't the refs disqualify him?"

"Sometimes they did. He got lots of warnings, and a bad reputation. But when he was warned and managed to choke it back, it was like putting dynamite in a bottle. He wouldn't sleep, he wouldn't eat, his heart would start racing, he would puke his guts out between rounds, and doctors had to be called to calm him down. I saw him do some things you wouldn't believe. He lost a match in Cincinnati, and instead of knock-ing over his king he bit it in half. I think he cracked a couple of teeth." It was true—two of my father's molars had given him lots of problems over the years, and he had recently had ex-pensive implants. "In Montreal, I saw him kick over a table and nearly break his opponent's legs. In San Francisco, he blundered badly and had to be wrestled off the hotel roof by the police. I think he would have thrown himself off."

With a sinking heart, I remembered the open window in our suite. "What happened to Stanwick?"

"That was a one-off tournament in Texas. An oil billionaire put up thirty thousand dollars for first place. Your father was undefeated till the last round, but he was really in bad shape. He was talking to himself and to opponents, he wasn't eating or sleeping, and then in his final game against Stanwick he threatened to kill him."

"It couldn't have been a real threat," I said. "My dad says chess is war."

"Chess is war, but it was a real threat," Liszt told me.

"How can you be sure?"

"Because when the ref heard it and disqualified Morris, he dove over the table and started choking poor Stanwick! I know because I was just two boards down. A bunch of us tried to pull him off, but it was like he was possessed. He was shrieking and frothing at the mouth, and he had the strength of five men. When we finally wrestled him off, Stanwick was unconscious. His neck was badly sprained—another few seconds and your father would have broken it, and Stanwick might very well have been paralyzed for life."

I winced.

"They took Stanwick out of that tournament room completely immobilized on a backboard," Liszt said, "with a cervical collar, like a player after a football injury. The hall was silent. I've played in chess tournaments my whole life and I've never seen anything like it."

"What happened to my dad?"

"While we were trying to save Stanwick, Morris ran back to his hotel room. The police went looking for him, but he had barricaded himself in. They broke down the door and found the room destroyed. Thousands and thousands of dollars' worth of damage. Mirrors cracked, windows broken—"

"Okay," I said. "That's enough."

I tried to stand, but Liszt leaned across the table and held me. "You need to hear this. He tried to kill himself. He locked himself in the bathroom and tried to hang himself with his belt. They cut him down and saved his life and took him to a hospital. I heard they were thinking of prosecuting him for assault, and I would have testified against him, but they decided he was insane and he ended up in the loony bin. And I guess you know the rest of the story."

He let me go and I sat there in the coffee shop, imagining my father choking some poor kid, and then all alone in a hotel bathroom, trying to hang himself.

"Get him out of here," Liszt whispered. "If you love him, go home. I'm seeing familiar signs. He's started talking to himself again. He's taking his pulse all the time. His heart is racing. History will repeat itself."

I swallowed but didn't say anything.

He finished his latte and crumpled the cup in a giant paw of a hand. "I never cared for your father. But you seem like a nice kid. He has a lot to be thankful for. So hear this warning loud and clear. If your dad stays at this tournament and somehow keeps winning, it's likely our paths will cross near the end. I know all his weaknesses. I need this prize money. Chess is war—I'll do whatever I need to do to win."

18

They don't normally let you back into a chess tournament's playing area once you've finished your game and left. I told the monitor at the door that my father was sick and I needed to see him right away. I think she could see how worried I was, and her face softened. She waved me through and whispered: "Please be quiet and quick."

My first impulse was to rip Dad out of there, march him to our car, and hightail it back to New Jersey while he was still relatively sane and healthy. But as I walked past the long tables of silent, concentrating chess players, I felt my resolve slipping.

I could see my dad now, up on the grandmasters' platform—arms folded, eyes on the board—looking calm and under control and not about to strangle anyone or leap out a window. Was he really in imminent danger of falling apart? What could I possibly say to get him to resign a tight game against a master? I felt myself slowing down with each step and realized I didn't have the nerve to make a big scene by insisting that he leave right now.

A game ended near me, and as the two players stood and shook hands I saw that one of them was Dr. Chisolm. I guessed from his tight, angry face that he had just lost. He marched to the scorer's table, and then headed out. "Dr. Chisolm," I called, following him, but he was already out the door and stalking toward the elevator with long and furious strides, as if he had lost a patient on the operating table and needed to run twenty laps or punch a heavy bag to let out his frustration.

I hurried after him and caught his arm. "Dr. Chisolm. I need to talk to you."

"Not now," he muttered. "Damn it, I should have won that one. Give me some space, Daniel." He tried to yank free, but I held on tight.

"Please," I said. "It's about my dad."

He stopped trying to pull away. "What's wrong?"

"He may need a doctor."

"Is he sick?"

I didn't have a sensible answer to that question. "Kind of. Or at least I think he will be."

"You think he will be?" Dr. Chisolm repeated, looking a little mystified, and then he led me through the common area to a quiet corner, near a marble fountain. The cascading water masked our words. "What's going on?"

I looked back at him and remembered the previous night at the steak restaurant when he had insulted my dad. Now I was thinking of trusting him with my father's deepest secret. I hesitated and pulled away from him, but I had no place to go and no one else to tell. I was surprised to feel hot tears squeezing out of my eyes and running down my cheeks. I hadn't cried in years, and I was deeply embarrassed, but I just couldn't stop. "I'm sorry," I said. "I—I just don't know what to do."

Dr. Chisolm sat me down on a bench and put his hand on my shoulder. All his anger at his chess loss seemed suddenly gone, and he looked reassuring and focused and even gentle. "Talk to me, Daniel. Anything you say will remain between us, in the strictest confidence. The more you tell me, the more I can help."

I didn't tell him everything, but I told him a lot. He listened silently till I was done, and then he said, "You absolutely did the right thing to tell me this. Has your father ever had a heart attack?"

"No," I answered.

"Chest pains? Shortness of breath?"

"Not that I know of. But he takes pills for high blood pressure. And he checks his pressure once a day."

"So do I," Dr. Chisolm said.

"He hasn't eaten much of anything at this tournament," I said. "Last night he barely touched his steak, and he didn't have any breakfast. And I don't think he's sleeping at all either."

"Your father's still a relatively young man," Dr. Chisolm pointed out. "He's a bit overweight, but he's aware of his past problems, and it sounds like he's monitoring himself. He should be able to handle a three-day chess tournament. I'll keep an eye on him, but I think he's going to be fine, so you should relax and give yourself a break. Okay?"

"Okay," I said. "Thanks."

He produced a handkerchief from a pocket and handed it to me. As I dabbed at my eyes he went on speaking in a soft, calm voice, staring off beyond me at the water splashing down into the fountain. "It sounds like the guy you just talked to was a jerk, digging up mud from thirty years ago that could only scare you. I'm not a psychologist, but your dad wouldn't be here unless he felt he could handle this. Sometimes it can be a very healthy thing to face one's old demons. Now," he said, "give me back my handkerchief and try to buck up, because here comes the grandmaster."

I saw that my dad had just walked out of the tournament hall and was standing next to Liu's mom, chatting with her and looking around. He spotted me, waved, and headed right over. I just had time to slip the handkerchief back into Dr. Chisolm's hand.

"Hey, Daniel," Dad said, "how'd the game go?"

"I won," I told him. "What about you?"

"It was essentially a drawn position, but Voorhees got greedy and overplayed it, and I made him pay."

As we talked, I noticed that Dr. Chisolm was taking a long, careful look at my father.

My dad, in turn, was studying me. "What's wrong?"

"What do you mean?"

"Your eyes are red. You don't look so good."

I shrugged. "Allergies."

"Since when do you have allergies?"

"It's probably all the dust in the carpets," Dr. Chisolm suggested, helping me out. "Makes my eyes red and puffy, too."

"Daniel, if you want to pass on that fancy French dinner, we have another offer," my father told me. "Your new friend and her mom want us to go with them to some karaoke place they know. It sounds like it might be fun and relaxing."

I glanced at Dr. Chisolm, who gave me a slight nod—fun and relaxing was what my father needed. "Let's do it," I said. I rubbed my eyes, which were still damp, and saw my dad watching me closely. "The tournament jitters must be getting to me a little," I said, turning things around so that I had an excuse Dad would understand.

"They get to everyone," he noted. "You just have to keep cool and gut it out. Take it from an old hand, if you let the pressure get to you, you can explode. Right, Sam?"

"Let's hope nobody explodes this weekend," Dr. Chisolm replied, and he looked just a little worried.

19

Dad was in his bedroom, and I was in our suite's living room watching a basketball game when my cell phone rang. I saw that it was my mom, and realized that in the whirlwind of the chess tournament I hadn't called her even once. I grabbed it quickly. "Hi, Mom."

"So you remember who I am?" she asked.

"Sorry. It's been a little crazy. How are things there?"

"Unchanged. Quiet. Except for your sister, who is always talking. She may be the first person to wear out a new cell phone in one week. Tell me about the chess tournament. Has it been crazy in a good way?"

I found myself telling her about everything except what I knew she was most interested in. "The room is incredible. We were upgraded to a suite. I'm talking to you looking out a window at the Hudson River and New Jersey. If you wave your hand I can probably see you. Oh, and our team was in first place after round one. We went out for a big steak dinner last night to celebrate. And, Mom, I just won a game."

"Congratulations," she said. "It sounds like you're living the high life. So, how's your father?"

I didn't know what to say. I was afraid of worrying her for nothing, but I also didn't want to hide the situation from her. Should I tell her about George Liszt's warnings, or trust Dr. Chisolm's reassurances? "He's in the next room," I finally mumbled. "Do you want me to put him on?"

"If I wanted to talk to your father, I would have called *him*. The reason I'm calling you is that I want a full and independent report. Is he enjoying himself?"

"I think so," I said truthfully. "He won his first two games. And we're spending more time together than we have in years. When you get him away from work, he's a pretty good guy."

"Do you think I would have married a louse?" she joked, but I could tell she was glad that my dad and I were having this time together.

"He's an incredible chess player. People still remember him from thirty years ago. He finished second in a U.S. Open. That's a giant chess tournament, open to everyone in the United States."

"Really? Who knew?" she said in wonder. "So is the secret chess champion I married taking care of himself?"

Just at that moment, a loud lowing came from the bedroom. Dad was doing one of his relaxation exercises, and it sounded like a stressed-out bull trying to escape from a fenced-in pasture.

"He's trying to," I hedged, covering the receiver with my hand so she wouldn't hear the weird sounds. "We're all doing what we can."

"Daniel? I'm not asking you if he's brushing his teeth regularly. I want to know if he's healthy."

I paced across the room, away from my dad's bedroom, holding the phone tightly to my ear. "Mom, these tournaments are a little hectic. What do you want me to say?"

"The full truth and nothing but the truth. I can tell that something's wrong. What exactly does 'hectic' mean? Is he eating, sleeping, and keeping calm?"

"No," I admitted. "He's not eating much, but it's only three days so he'll lose a little weight and come out fine. And I don't think he's sleeping too well. But nobody sleeps in a chess tournament."

"Why not?" she demanded, sounding more and more worried. "I thought you had a hotel suite. Doesn't it have big, comfortable beds?"

"Yes, but there's a lot of pressure."

My father's voice floated out from the bedroom. I guess he had finished his exercises. "Daniel, are you ready to go to lunch?"

"In a minute," I shouted back. "I need to change my shirt." I headed into my bedroom and closed the door.

"What's the matter with your shirt?" Mom asked.

"Nothing," I told her. "Listen, we're going to lunch. I can't talk too much more. I think everything's going to be fine here. We have a doctor on the team. I asked him to keep an eye on Dad."

"What kind of doctor?"

I had told her to reassure her, but now I regretted it. "He's a cardiologist," I admitted.

"Oh my God," she said. "What's wrong with his heart?"

"Nothing. I'm just trying to be careful. The doctor said not to worry. He thinks Dad's fine."

"Daniel, *what are you not telling me*?"

My father had walked into the living room and he sounded a little impatient as he knocked on my bedroom door. "How much time does it take to change a shirt? We're going to be late for lunch, and the next round starts right after that."

"Coming," I shouted out to him. Then, into the phone, I whispered: "Mom, I've really gotta go."

"Don't hang up on me," she ordered. "We're not finished yet. I need to know what's going on . . ."

I kept my voice low, and gave it to her fast. "Okay, here's the truth. Years ago when he was a kid he couldn't handle this kind of pressure. That's why he gave up chess. Now he thinks he can, and the doctor thinks so, too, so to hell with George Liszt, and I really have to go to lunch."

"Daniel, who is George Liszt? Why do you have to go to lunch so urgently if your father's not eating anything?"

"Don't worry, Mom. I'll call you in a little," I said and clicked off the phone. I pulled on a new shirt and walked out into the living room. Dad was standing by the window, check-ing his blood pressure with a little device he carries with him. "How's the old blood pressure?" I asked.

"Elevated," he told me. "Who was that on the phone?"

"Liu," I mumbled.

"Don't lie to me," he said. "It was your mother, checking up on me. What did you tell her?"

"That you weren't eating or sleeping well, but we were hav-ing a good time and we would get through this okay."

He considered and nodded. "That sounds about right. Don't tell her too much, Daniel. She does tend to worry. And I'm sure you now know some things that would turn her hair white."

I wasn't sure exactly what he meant by that, but I suddenly felt very uneasy.

Dad turned from the window. His black eyes were on me suddenly, boring into me. "I happened to glance up from my game with Voorhees and saw you leaving the tournament room with my old friend George Liszt."

I froze, looked right back at him, and slowly nodded. "It wasn't my idea," I said. "He sought me out and said he had to tell me something . . . critical."

"I'm not blaming you. But I am curious. Why did you feel like you needed to hear him out?"

"He said he wanted to give me a warning," I explained softly. "I felt I had to hear it. I just want to make sure you're going to be okay." I paused for a second and met his eyes. "I got you into this. I feel responsible."

"You're not," Dad said. "But I wouldn't make a habit of talking to George. He has his own agenda."

"He told me that. He said that if you and he meet in the final round he's going to press all your buttons and do whatever it takes to win."

Dad nodded. "I have no doubt of that. But it won't come to that, Daniel. I'll lose well before that final game. I almost dropped a point to Voorhees."

"But you didn't," I pointed out.

Dad looked back at me and put his hands in his pockets. "True," he said. "That's one thing about chess tournaments—you can never tell." Suddenly I saw a ferocious gleam in his eye. "George always had a strong intuition about these things. He must be sensing something." Dad's lips twisted up into a very slight smile, and he threw back his shoulders as if accepting a challenge. "Understand this, Daniel—the only reason he talked to you and tried to scare us away is that he's starting to feel a little bit nervous. And if it does come to that, I'll meet him in open combat and I won't back off."

20

"So, how do you two know each other?" Britney asked Liu, poking a piece of lettuce around her plate.

"I kicked his butt in the first round, and then I felt sorry for him," Liu answered, and bit into a double cheeseburger. "Hey, Daniel, stop eating all the french fries."

"You're the one wolfing them down two at a time," I pointed out. We were splitting a large order, and I was positive she had eaten twice as many of them as I had. "Want one?" I asked Britney.

"No thanks," Britney said. "You guys enjoy them." For some reason it seemed like she couldn't stop watching Liu and me.

We were all eating lunch together at a burger joint across from the hotel—the Mind Cripplers, Mariel and Britney, who had finished up at the spa, and Liu and her mom. Liu and her mother had won their first two games, and Liu's mom was in a grand mood. "Our team is boring," she explained to Mariel.

"It's no fun eating with chess-nerd vegans. Liu needed a burger to recharge her batteries, so I said, 'I bet those Mind Cripplers know how to chow down.' All except for Morris, that is."

"I don't eat much during a tournament," my dad told her. He had seemed in good spirits when he defeated Voorhees, but now he looked like the pressure and the lack of sleep were catching up to him. He hadn't eaten a crumb for breakfast and he was passing on lunch. His eyes had deep circles under them, and as he sat there he drummed his fingers nervously on the table.

"Well, you'd better work up an appetite for tonight," Mr. Kinney said. "Chez André doesn't serve finger food."

"As a matter of fact," Dad told him, "Daniel and I are going to pass. We've been invited to a karaoke place."

Mr. Kinney looked back at him. "Tonight is the last evening of the tournament. I really think our team needs to stay together and strategize."

"And the food at Chez André is divine," Mariel contributed.

"Divine or not, we've made our decision," my dad told Randolph. "You guys go and have some foie gras for us."

"Let them go," Brad said to his father. "There's no reason we have to do everything together. Britney and I were thinking we might split off after dinner and check out some music."

Britney looked surprised by this news.

"The night before our last round you're not going out clubbing, so you can forget that," Mr. Kinney told his son.

Brad smiled back at his father, but not a very friendly smile. "Thanks for the advice. I will think about it."

"I said no," Randolph told him.

Brad half stood, squared his broad shoulders, and glared back at his father. "I'm eighteen, Dad. My decision, not yours."

Liu whispered to me, "Boy, your team is *really* more interesting than ours."

"You'll do what I say," Mr. Kinney told Brad, "and right now that means park your butt in your seat and zip your lip, or I guarantee you'll regret it."

Brad didn't sit down. He looked like he wanted to take on his father, who for his part was clearly ready to tussle. Watching them, I wondered if they had ever come to blows in the past, and if so, who had won.

"Hey, everybody." Dr. Chisolm jumped in. "I have an idea."

His voice broke the impasse between the Kinneys, and we all turned to look at him. "I love fine French food as much as the next guy," he said, "but why don't we save Chez André for another time. If Grandmaster Pratzer doesn't mind us horning in on his plans, a light Japanese dinner and some karaoke sounds like it might be a little more healthy and relaxing. We could all stay together, the young members of our team could let loose and have a little fun, and I could demonstrate why I went into medicine instead of rock and roll."

I was a little surprised by his suggestion, and I wondered if it was at least partly spurred by his desire to keep a close eye on my father.

"Sounds good to me," Brad said. "Anything but a boring French meal." He sat down and took a big slurp of root beer.

"It's a shame about Chez André," Mariel chimed in, "but

I love Japanese food, too. And I have a little frock I can wear."

"It sounds like a plan, then," Dr. Chisolm said. "Randolph, are you okay with it?"

Mr. Kinney didn't look particularly happy, but he could tell that the tide had turned against his fancy French restaurant. He hesitated a long beat and then grunted, "Okay, then. If Morris doesn't mind us barging in on his night out?"

Dad glanced at me and I gave him a covert nod. "It's fine with me," he said. "Mabel? This was your idea."

Liu's mom looked around the table and opened her arms wide. "The more Mind Cripplers the merrier," she said, and there was a mischievous twinkle in her eye, as if she knew exactly what she was getting into and welcomed the insanity. "You let my daughter and me join you for lunch. The least we can do is return the favor for dinner. Let's make a night of it. My only requirement is that we all have to really try to let our hair down and have some fun. Except for you, Morris," she said with a teasing smile. "I mean the hair part."

I was a little surprised—I had never seen anyone flirt with my father before.

"Mom!" Liu said.

"It's okay," my father replied, smiling back at Liu's mom. "I may be bald, but wait till you see me do Elvis."

21

The middle rounds of a chess tournament are a grind. The opening day excitement is over. The final-day glory is yet to come. Sandwiched in between are the middle rounds, when tired minds are stretched to the breaking point.

You could see the pressure taking its toll. Red eyes crawled from boards to score sheets, sore backs slouched in uncomfortable folding chairs, openings were misplayed and middle games squandered as exhausted players blundered away pawns and then slammed chess clocks like they really wanted to slug their opponents.

I kept expecting my father to make a mistake or shout at his opponent and get disqualified. But he hung in there— when it came to chess it was like he had an iron will and reserves of energy. Then again, I think he had a special reason for not wanting to lose to his third-round opponent.

Dad was matched against a guy named Hutchinson, who

had a child's body and an adult's serious face. He was twelve, but he looked like he was nine. "Prodigy," people whispered. "Pint-size wrecking ball. Could become the strongest American player in years. He won the New York Elementary Title. He's jumped five hundred rating points in the last three months. This kid is the real deal."

When Hutchinson sat down opposite my dad, it was like an older and a younger version of the same person coming face to face. The twelve-year-old propped himself up on a pillow to get a better view of the board, thumped his thin elbows down on the table, and folded his wrists together just the way my dad did.

For all the kid's chess success, there seemed to me to be something very sad about Hutchinson—he looked so lonely and precocious sitting up on that dais with the adult grandmasters, scrunching up his face in concentration and attacking fury. My father looked back at him and I could tell Dad was remembering how it felt to be a young hotshot, and all the reasons he had given up the game.

It was a battle between age and youth, a former prodigy and the new up-and-comer. Hutchinson threw down the gauntlet and attacked right from the start, and Dad leaned slightly forward in his seat, pushed his glasses up on his nose, and accepted the challenge, defending carefully with the black pieces.

I would have liked to watch more of their game, but my own third-round opponent was the expert who had been intimidated and destroyed by George Liszt in the previous round in just fifteen moves. His name was Owen Burghoff, and he sure wasn't intimidated by me.

We had each won a game and lost one, but Burghoff clearly felt he didn't belong so far back, playing such a low-rated opponent. From the moment he sauntered up I could see that he was determined to clobber me quickly and climb back into the upper brackets of this tournament.

He was a fussy dude—overdressed in a gray sports jacket. When he arrived at the table I held out my hand for a shake but he pretended not to see it. While we waited for the command to start our clock, I tried to make polite conversation, but he gave me one glance and then completely ignored me. He took off his expensive watch and laid it down exactly parallel to the edge of the chessboard, checked the lead in his mechanical pencil, and filled out his score sheet in small, perfectly formed letters.

I hated his manners and decided not to go quietly. I knew I couldn't beat an expert, but maybe I could make him sweat a little. I got through the opening on fairly even terms but dropped a pawn in the middle game, and then I lost a second pawn. Burghoff pressed his advantage and kept glancing impatiently across the table at me, as if waiting for me to give up. He hissed at me at one point: "You have no chance. End this with dignity and resign."

I probably would have given up against anyone else, but I had taken such a dislike to this guy that I decided to make him sit there and wait. "Don't talk to me during the game or

I'll have to call over a ref," I warned him. I took my time on a bunch of fairly obvious moves, and got up to watch my dad because I could tell that if I left the table it would really irritate Burghoff.

Dad looked like he had imploded. He had sunk deep into himself, and his whole body seemed to be trembling, as if his heartbeat was shaking his extremities. But he had absorbed all of Hutchinson's best shots, and now he was slowly tightening his defensive position, like a boa constrictor choking the breath out of a pesky rodent before devouring it.

"Your dad will win this game," Grandmaster Liszt whispered as I passed, "but at what cost? Look at him, Daniel! Do yourselves both a favor and get him out of here before it's too late."

"Worry about yourself," I told him. I returned to my own table, took eight minutes to study my obviously lost position, and finally made a move that I could have made in ten seconds. Burghoff rolled his eyes as if to say "Finally" and immediately made his own highly aggressive move. He intended to finish me off and get out of there.

Suddenly I saw it. He had moved too quickly and left himself open to a combination that would win his queen. I made the right move, and he saw what he had fallen into. His body went rigid, as if someone had poured concrete down his spine. He took twenty minutes on his next move, and fifteen on the one after that, searching the board as if looking for a hidden cave beneath the squares where his queen could flee to and escape. But there was no cave, no way out, and eventually he had to make the forced move. I reached across the board and took his queen.

Suddenly I was flooded with so much energy I could barely sit still or think straight. I was a queen up against an expert! "Don't give it back," I cautioned myself. "Don't choke. Just play smart." Burghoff thrashed and squirmed and set traps and tried for counterplay, but a queen up is a queen up, and the game was soon over. He didn't shake my hand after the game either—he just stood up in a huff, grabbed his fancy watch, and stalked off.

I felt a tug on my arm. It was Liu. She looked really impressed. "Did you actually beat that guy?" she asked.

"Yeah, I toasted an expert. How about that?" I asked.

"Not bad," she said.

"Not bad at all," my dad seconded. He was standing on my other side, smiling at me proudly.

"I assume you beat the young brat?" I asked him.

Dad nodded. "Spanked him and sent him to bed without any supper."

"Sounds like we may have some reasons to celebrate tonight," Liu said.

"Not so fast," Dad cautioned her. "We still have to get through the dreaded fourth round."

My father's warning proved prophetic. I came apart in the fourth round and lost very quickly. I was tired from the last game, and my opponent—a kid named Gajanand, who was playing on a team from one of the elite New York public high schools—destroyed me. Still, two and two was a very credible score to finish the second day.

Eric dropped his second game and was also two and two. Brad had won two games, drawn a game, and lost a game, so he was a half point ahead of me at two and a half and one and a half. Dr. Chisolm and Mr. Kinney had won three games and lost one. So all in all, the Mind Cripplers were doing pretty well and were positioned to win the tournament if two things happened. First, we had to do well in the final round. And second, my father had to win his fourth game.

If chess was really war, there was murder and mayhem going on up on the dais—the patzers and the prodigies and the overambitious experts and masters had been sent packing and now the grandmasters were starting to face off. There had been five of them when the tournament started, but one of them—Grandmaster Murray—had drawn a game with a master. That left four undefeated grandmasters going into the final two games: my dad and George Liszt, and Grandmaster Sanchez and Grandmaster Leshkin.

In the fourth round, my dad was paired with Grandmaster Sanchez, the top-rated player in this entire tournament at 2620. I had heard from the tournament gossip mill that Sanchez was one of the strongest players in America and frequently played in international tournaments. He was a small, dignified man in his late thirties, with a calm, polite manner that vanished when he sat down at the chessboard.

It made me feel proud that my father was up on the dais this late in the tournament, matched on fairly even terms with one of the strongest chess players in America. A live feed of the grandmaster games played on large monitor screens out in the common area. I could see my dad and Grandmaster Sanchez concentrating intently, and each time they moved the growing crowd reacted and kibbitzed.

My dad had the white pieces, and I was surprised to see him start off with the Giuoco Piano, the very opening he had cautioned me never to play against stronger players because all its major lines have been analyzed to death. His fourth move brought gasps from the spectators as he moved up his knight pawn, offering it as a sacrifice. I watched on the monitor as Grandmaster Sanchez looked across the board at him, smiled slightly as if to say: "Are you serious?" and then took the pawn.

"I can't believe he's playing that!" a tall man near me said.

"What is it?" I asked.

"The Evans Gambit," the tall man explained. "It was one of the most popular openings two hundred years ago. All the great old masters played it—de la Bourdonnais, Anderssen, and of course Morphy. But no one plays it anymore."

I had to smile. My father, aware that he hadn't kept up with the latest advances in chess theory and facing a top young grandmaster, was channeling his boyhood hero, Paul Morphy, and playing a very old opening.

"That's not quite true," a studious-looking teenager told

the tall man. "Nunn and Timman played the Evans Gambit thirty years ago."

The tall man shrugged dismissively. "Nunn and Timman? Hardly a revival."

"And Kasparov defeated Anand with it in 1995," a man with an authoritative English accent pointed out. "It's never been completely refuted."

The crowd grew from fifteen or twenty to thirty, and then to fifty. On the other monitor, I could see George Liszt locked in a tight positional battle with Grandmaster Leshkin.

One by one the Mind Cripplers joined me till our whole team was there, watching. The Evans Gambit put my father down a pawn, but gave him a wide-open attacking game. Both his bishops were soon sweeping long diagonals, and his king was safely castled while the black king was stuck in the center of the board.

I don't think I've ever been more nervous and at the same time more proud of my dad than I was in that hour when he attacked Grandmaster Sanchez with everything he had. The challenge brought out his very best, both in chess and also physically. He was obviously exhausted, but the game energized him. They sat facing each other, concentrating deeply and not saying a word or moving a muscle. They were both completely locked in, going at it with everything they had.

I finally understood what my father had meant back in our home in New Jersey when he told me that true chess was not replaying memorized openings or stale variations but mental combat—two minds in unfamiliar territory, wrestling with each other. Grandmaster Sanchez played a hitherto untried line at move nine, and he and Dad were soon far off down their own unexplored road, with no maps from the past to guide them.

My Mind Crippler teammates were rooting for my father as he sacrificed yet another pawn, and then a knight, to press his attack. "That's it, Morry, hit him with the kitchen sink," Randolph enthused, fists clenched.

"Your dad's a freaking badass giant deep-sea octopus!" Eric said, clapping me on the back. "Look at those tentacles."

Grandmaster Sanchez took a long time on his twenty-ninth move, and an even longer time on his thirtieth. I couldn't completely decipher the position, but it was clear that he was worried. The whispers in the lobby swung back and forth: "He's got this defended." "No, he's toast." "No way Sanchez is going to get caught in some mating net. He's a world-class player." "World class or not, he's not getting out of this one alive."

I stood there watching my father, and I was sweating profusely in the air-conditioned hall. My knees felt weak, and my hands were clasped tightly, as if some team prayer might help. But I wasn't praying—I was watching my father do what he was best at, after a lifetime of hiding his talent. Maybe every kid deserves to see his father be a hero just once, for a few minutes.

Liu seemed to understand how I felt—she stood next to me and propped me up slightly with her right hand touching my shoulder. "He's incredible," she whispered, and it was so strange to hear someone say that about my bald, potbellied accountant of a father.

"Check," my father said, when Sanchez finally made his thirtieth move.

This time Sanchez barely hesitated. He stood up and offered his hand. My dad shook it and finally smiled.

Suddenly people were applauding all around me, and my teammates were congratulating me as if I had done something extraordinary. But I was hurrying toward the doors to the tournament hall. The crowd was thick in front of me and I had to fight my way through it, so I reached the double doors just as my father walked out, carrying his score sheet. He saw me and smiled. "Hey, how about that?"

I opened my arms and we embraced. "You were . . . stupendous," I told him. I felt the cold sweat all over him, and also that he was trembling. "Are you okay?" I asked him.

"Sure," he said, and then he passed out in my arms.

22

The EMTs had gone and Dr. Chisolm had finished his own examination, and now Dad lay on his bed in our suite with his legs propped up on pillows so that his head was lower than his knees. He was taking occasional sips of bottled water, breathing in through his nostrils and exhaling from his mouth, and trying to make a joke out of the whole thing. "That's what happens when you beat somebody over 2600," he said. "And if you beat someone over 2700 your nose falls off your face."

"Well, your nose is still fastened in the right place, but it wouldn't hurt you to go to an emergency room," Dr. Chisolm told him. "Just to be safe. They can run some tests on you that I can't run here . . ."

"You checked out my heart, and the ambulance guys ran plenty of tests," Dad told him. "I feel fine now. It was just nerves. It's happened before. If I go to an emergency room I'm gonna sit there for half the night waiting to be seen, and then they'll keep me for observation. I won't be in any shape to finish the tournament tomorrow."

"I'm not sure you should play tomorrow," Mr. Kinney told him. "Much as I'd like to win this thing."

"I'm playing," Dad said softly but with determination. "I've come too far. I'm not backing down." He glanced at Dr. Chisolm. "My heart's fine, right, Sam?"

"I see no sign of arrhythmia, or any other cardiac condition," Dr. Chisolm admitted. "You say you have a history of anxiety-related fainting. The fact that you remember seeing spots just before you collapsed is an indication of reduced blood flow to the brain, which can certainly be caused by an extreme nervous reaction. But all that being said, Morris, we need to err on the side of safety."

"Listen to Dr. Chisolm," I urged my father. "Be safe. To hell with the tournament. Let's run every test, stay the night in a hospital, and then go home. That's what Mom said we should do . . ."

"No way I'm spending tonight in a hospital and no way I'm going home early," my father declared resolutely. Then he smiled at me and took my hand, and he really did look much better. "Look, Daniel, I understand that you're worried, but I've had this before, and it passes. I know my own body. Let's go do the karaoke party. What I need is to relax and sing a little Elvis."

"Forget the karoke," Dr. Chisolm told him. "At the very

least you should stay in the hotel and rest. We can order something healthy from room service."

Dad sat up in bed, looking and sounding a bit like a rebellious child who was refusing to take his medicine. "I don't want hotel food. And I *really* need to take my mind off chess for a little while. I appreciate all your concern, but we made a plan and let's stick to it." He looked at Liu's mother, who was part of the small throng of team members and concerned friends that had gathered in our hotel suite. "We have a reservation at Lucky Hana's Hall of Karaoke for nine p.m., right?"

"I canceled that, Morris," Liu's mom said. "We'll do it another time."

"Uncancel it," he snapped. "I want to go. This is just silly." He stood up from the bed and looked around. "Where's my jacket? Daniel, are you ready?"

"We're not leaving this hotel, unless we head to a hospital," I told him.

He looked back at me and then at the other people in the suite, and there was a long, silent impasse.

"I've got an idea," Randolph finally said. "Why don't we do the karaoke party right here at the Palace Royale? We can set it up in my suite and bring in some Japanese food."

"Where are you going to rent a karaoke machine at this hour?" Liu's mother asked.

"Leave that to me," Mr. Kinney told her. "This is Manhattan. For the right price, you can get anything, day or night. What do you say, Morris?"

Dad seemed inclined to argue, but then he sat back down on his bed. "Deal," he said. "Just make sure you get a good sound system."

I went into my own bedroom and called Mom again. I knew she was standing by, and sure enough she answered at the first ring. "He seems much better," I told her.

"Let the hospital decide that," she said.

"He refuses to go to a hospital."

"Refuse to let him refuse," she ordered.

"Mom, I can't force him. He's walking around and he seems to have an appetite. He's agreed to rest. We're going to have dinner here in the hotel. If Dr. Chisolm thought there was any danger of a real health emergency, he wouldn't let Dad do this."

Mom didn't sound convinced—she sounded angry. "Put your father on."

I walked into Dad's bedroom and offered him the phone. He knew from my face who was on the line. "Hi, Ruth," he said. "I guess you heard that I had a little hiccup, but I'm fine and there's no need to be concerned . . ."

That was all he got to say. After that he just listened, and I could hear her raised voice crackling over the phone and the word "hospital" repeated several times. Finally, Mom ran out of words.

"Okay, Ruth, I'll think about it and call you later," Dad told her. "Try not to worry. Love you." Before she could respond and give him another earful, he hung up and handed me back the phone. "You're just worrying her for nothing." Then he turned to Mr. Kinney. "When you order the food, can you get me some edamame? They're Japanese green soybeans . . ."

"I know what edamame are," Brad's dad told him. "Leave the ordering to me. You just take care of yourself."

23

Lights flashed and music thumped—the Kinneys' suite had been transformed into party central. Not only had Randolph rented an impressive karaoke machine with a monitor that showed the lyrics of the songs, but he must have paid Lucky Hana's to throw in some decorations. There were paper dragons taped to the walls and rainbow streamers fluttering down from the ceiling. A disco ball dangled from a light fixture in the center of the room and cast whirling reflections on the white walls.

"Now, *this* is the way to take your mind off chess," my father said with a smile as we walked in through the door. "Thanks for going to all the trouble, Randolph."

"No trouble at all," our host said. "I had Hana's deliver the stuff and some guys from the hotel set it up. They said since we're at the end of a hallway we can get pretty loud without bothering other rooms. There are two big bowls of edamame over there on the table, Grandmaster," he told my dad. "How are you feeling?"

"Much better. Are you sure you ordered enough sushi?" my father asked him with a grin. "I think there must be one or two kinds of fish you left out."

"I doubt it," Mr. Kinney said. "I told them to bring the whole menu. Don't be polite, guys. Dig in."

A buffet of sushi had been arranged on a fleet of miniature wooden boats on the tables. I followed my father to the food, and just as I reached out for a salmon roll I heard a loud guitar riff, and then a deep voice boomed out: *"I can't get no . . . satisfaction."*

The karaoke machine sat on an end table in a corner of the room, with two lamps pointing at it for improvised spotlights. Brad stood with the microphone in his hand, belting out a surprisingly good rendition of "Satisfaction." He might not have been Mick Jagger, but in addition to being a swimming champion, a chess master, and a lady-killer, he could carry a tune and he even had the prancing, cocksure dance moves of a rock star.

He paused after the first verse and pointed at my dad. "Yo, undefeated Grandmaster, this one's for you and the rest of the dads—from the Dark Ages of rock and roll, when you guys were young and cool and had some hair."

"I was young and I had some hair but I was never cool," Dad responded, but Brad drowned him out with another burst of "I can't get no satisfaction." He strutted forward, did a few pelvic grinds, and stuck his chin out like a bad-boy rock idol.

Britney sat on a chair a few feet away, watching Brad's every hair flip and hip gyration. She was wearing short shorts and a halter top, and when he finished his song she jumped up and clapped. "That was great!"

"I'm just getting warmed up," he told her. "Hey, Danny boy. It turns out you play chess a little better than we thought. Do you sing?"

"Like a frog," I told him.

"Go ahead and try," Britney encouraged me.

"If he's a frog, then he's a frog," Brad said dismissively. "I'm gonna sing another one. Hey, Brit, grab me one of those inside-out rolls."

"You better not be a frog," Liu told me, walking up, "because we're on for a duet later and I don't partner with amphibians." She also looked hot, in dark stretch leggings, a long black T-shirt, and a gold chain belt.

"Can you sing?" I asked her.

"What do you think, Jersey boy?"

"Better than you can play chess?" I probed.

She flashed me a flirtatious smile. "You'll find out before the evening is over."

"I like your outfit," Britney told Liu. "That's a really cool belt."

Liu looked back at her a little puzzled, as if she wanted to dislike Britney but couldn't find a reason to do it. "Thanks. Where did you get those shorts?"

"At a boutique in the Village today. They have lots of great stuff. I can give you the address."

The room filled up as Liu's mother, Dr. Chisolm, and Eric arrived, and everyone began eating and taking turns singing. Last to show up was Britney's mom, Mariel, resplendent in a red silk sleeveless dress and wearing a necklace with a large pendant of diamonds that flashed as brightly as the disco ball. She made a grand entrance, swishing in with a room service waiter right behind her who wheeled a cart with several bottles of champagne on ice.

While the waiter opened the champagne, Mariel took the microphone from Eric, who was in the middle of a song. He surrendered the mic without a struggle, and the music shut off. "Don't stop the party for me," she announced, while completely stopping the party. "But I just wanted to say how much it means to Britney and me that you included us in your little soiree. Men haven't always treated me so nicely—" Mariel broke off for a second, just standing there smiling her thousand-watt smile.

"Mom," Britney said, and the one word was a warning and a not-so-gentle nudge to stay on message.

Mariel nodded to her daughter. "So we've brought some bubbly—just a taste for the kiddos and a little more for the grownups. Let's start things off the right way." The waiter had a dozen long-stemmed glasses on his cart, and he quickly poured for everyone. "Randolph, as our host, please give the toast," Mariel requested.

Randolph considered for a minute and then looked at my father. "Grandmaster Pratzer, you're the man tonight. What are we drinking to?"

My dad raised his glass. Given his team prayer, I expected him to say something like "family love" or "parents and kids," but instead he raised his champagne glass said in a loud voice that was almost warlike: "Ladies and gentlemen, confusion to the enemy!"

I raised my half glass of champagne and turned to Liu. "Confusion to the enemy, Catwoman."

"Kanpai, Mind Crippler, and son of Super Mind Crippler," she said back.

24

I was exhausted from the three chess games in one day and the added stress of worrying about my dad. The party in the Kinneys' suite seemed to whirl and flash around me like the disco ball overhead. Every once in a while the people in the room would snap back into sharp focus and I would glimpse a few seconds of strange behavior or notice a memorable karaoke performance.

Mariel floated through the suite like a beautiful red butterfly, alighting here and there, at one point touching my shoulder and saying: "I hear you won two games, Daniel. Britney is your number one fan." Then Mariel winked at me and whispered conspiratorially: "Just between us, your friend in black over there is absolutely stunning."

I blinked and Mariel was clear on the other side of the room, hand-feeding Mr. Kinney an eel-and-avocado roll and laughing at something he said. A minute later I glimpsed her on the throw-rug "stage" all alone, singing a haunting solo of "Hey Jude" in a husky whisper, her luminous blue eyes fixed on the suite's wide windows that looked down on the lights of Manhattan and the dark band of Hudson River that twisted away into blackness.

The room whirled and righted and I spotted my dad snacking on edamame and sipping his glass of champagne. "Careful, Morris," I heard Dr. Chisolm warn. "Those pills you took to relax shouldn't be mixed with alcohol."

"You also said I should have fun," Dad reminded him.

"I'll keep a close eye on the Grandmaster," Mabel promised Dr. Chisolm. "That's still his first glass."

Liu was standing next to me, also watching them. "It's weird," she whispered so that only I could hear, "but I think my mom likes your dad."

I wouldn't have said it out loud, but I couldn't deny it. "Truly weird," I admitted. "Where's *your* dad?"

"Dead," Liu replied in a hard, flat voice. "Heart attack. Three years ago. He died at his desk at work."

"I'm so sorry," I whispered back.

She shrugged. "Don't let anyone tell you that things happen for a reason. Life just sucks sometimes."

"It must have been really hard," I said softly.

She didn't say anything, but she turned away from me and I thought that maybe I now understood a little bit of where her tough exterior came from.

I didn't know what else to say or do so I put my hand

lightly on her back and whispered: "I'm sorry you had to go through that, Liu."

She turned back and I saw that her black eyes had teared up, and then they drew closer and suddenly she had leaned forward and kissed me lightly on the lips. "Thanks." She breathed. "Jersey boy." I felt the dampness of her tears on my cheek. We stayed close for a few seconds, and then Liu followed my eyes to our parents and said: "Don't look so worried, Daniel—my mom knows your father's married. She's just having a little fun."

The music thumped and the disco ball spun and suddenly I was eating sushi and listening to Mr. Kinney and Dr. Chisolm sing a raucous disco duet. They were showing off all kinds of corny moves from years past, as if trying to win the award for number one cheeseball act at the party.

Brad and Eric didn't seem to want to watch their dads sing. I noticed them vanish into one of the suite's bedrooms. I wasn't sure why till Brad came over a few minutes later to tell Liu and me that we were singing next. "You're on deck, Patzerface. Try not to croak too much."

We watched him saunter away, and he nearly tripped over a chair.

"Looks like he's having trouble navigating," Liu said.

"I bet he and Eric have a bottle stashed in his bedroom." Her lip wrinkled as if she had just tasted something unpleasant. "I don't like the way he treats that girl."

Brad had grabbed Britney for a slow dance. He looked

enormous swaying with her, his thick arms wrapped around her back. He half dragged her in a slow circle, and then suddenly demanded: "What the hell kind of music is this?"

My father was "onstage" with Mabel, doing his hammy rendition of "Heartbreak Hotel" while she danced and sang backup and looped a couple of Hawaiian leis around his neck. Dad was a little better at singing and moving his hips than he was at wiggling his ears. It was good to see him forgetting about chess for a few moments, but it was also a little weird—I had never seen him flirt with a woman besides my mom before. Come to think of it, I wasn't sure if I had ever seen him flirt with her either.

I understood it was harmless, but watching them laugh together made me wonder for the first time if my parents were really happy together, or if they were just going through the motions and responsibilities of keeping a house and raising kids. Had Dad settled into a safe life and routine, and was this strange tournament weekend knocking down all his defenses and barriers?

They finished and high-fived each other, and Brad motioned me up to the stage. "Next, for your listening pleasure, the princess who kissed the frog," he said.

Liu took my hand. "Ready?"

"I really hope you can sing," I whispered back.

"Remember when I told you I was mad at my mom for making me come to this tournament, because I was supposed to go to a concert with my friends?"

I nodded. "Yeah."

"Well, it wasn't a concert I was going to listen to," Liu said. "It was a concert I was singing at. My friends and I have a band, and I do the vocals. Let's nail this."

We walked onto the "stage" and I had a moment to think how surreal this was—I was getting ready to perform a duet with a girl I hadn't known two days ago, who had just kissed me. Her mother and my father were standing together watching us.

A week ago I had thought my dad was a dull accountant and a distant father. Now we had grown much closer and everyone called him Grandmaster and admired his brilliance. Meanwhile, the two coolest seniors at the Loon Lake Academy were whistling, stomping, and shouting, "Go for it, Patzer-face, show us what you got!"

Liu took a mic and handed me the other one. "I get the feeling you don't sing karaoke a lot?"

"That would be never," I admitted.

"Watch the words light up on the monitor and just come in on the choruses. I'll cue you. Here we go."

Liu had chosen "My Heart Will Go On," the theme song of the movie *Titanic*. After hearing it about a million times I hated that song more than just about any other. But then the music started up—flutes and recorders—and the first verse lit up on the monitor and Liu opened her mouth and something magical happened.

She was a fantastic singer—a natural. From the first word

out of her mouth, everyone in the room shut up and stared. She didn't dance around on the stage or make wild arm movements or flip her long hair—she just stayed in one place and sang her heart out. I got the feeling she was really singing about her father, and how much she missed him.

As she sang, I glanced at my own father and wondered how many more years would have gone by if we had not taken a chance on this weekend and started to understand and connect with each other.

Liu finished a verse and reached back for my hand. I put it in hers, and she pulled me forward as the words of the chorus came on the screen and lit up. Now I am not a good singer, but I understood how much courage it had taken for Liu to reveal so much of herself to a room full of strangers, and I did my best to forget all my fears and just plunge in. Her voice seemed to welcome me and wrap around my own, and prop me up and fill in the rough cracks and lead my shaky baritone in the right directions. The chorus ended and she gave my hand a squeeze and whispered, "You're no frog."

Then I stepped back and let her do her thing. When the second chorus came Liu reached back and took my hand again, and this time I was ready. But just as I stepped forward, the door to the Kinneys' suite opened. Two people hurried from the short hall into the living room, and I stopped singing. Liu went on till the end of the line and then whispered: "Come on, Daniel, you're doing great."

"Thanks," I said, "but we'd better stop." I clicked off the music. "Liu, I'd like you to meet my mother."

My mom stepped forward, looking concerned and a little angry, and I saw my sister, Kate, behind her. Mom took in the party room for a moment with its dragons and disco ball. She gave my dad a long look—his face was flushed, the Hawaiian leis were draped around his neck, and he clutched an empty champagne flute. Then, squinting in the flash of the disco ball, Mom peered at me, still holding Liu's hand. "Excuse me," she said, "but could someone tell me what is going on here?"

There was a moment of silence. Then my sister stepped out from behind my mom and asked: "Hey, are those California rolls? When do I get a chance to sing?"

25

This party was impossible to kill. It seemed to sweep on, with its own inner life and momentum. When my mom had stomped in, furious at my dad for staying when his health was in question and not exactly pleased with me for ignoring her commands to bring him home, I would have bet that would have derailed our karaoke soiree. But the disco ball flashed and I blinked, and the party seemed to have mysteriously gathered strength again, like a hurricane that has moved out over open water and regenerated.

There was Mom, accepting a drink from Mr. Kinney and a fried dumpling from Dr. Chisolm. "Your husband is a genius," Mr. Kinney told her. "A maestro."

"And we're watching him very carefully," Dr. Chisolm assured her. "Don't worry about a thing."

And there was my sister, who loves Japanese food, attacking the sushi buffet like a killer whale closing in on a reef teeming with fish. A few minutes later, Kate had taken the stage and was singing Katy Perry's "Firework" and throwing in her best hip-hop moves from summer camp.

I introduced Liu to my mom. "She's a seriously good chess player, Mom," I said. "And she's in a band, and she can sing like a real rock star."

Liu gave me a little smile and then took my mother's hand without a hint of shyness. "It's nice to meet you," she told my mother. "Your son's not so bad either."

"He's full of surprises," Mom agreed with a nod, studying Liu and, I think, liking what she saw. "But he doesn't always listen to his mother."

"That unfortunately sounds pretty normal," Liu's own mother commented, stepping up to say hello. "If my daughter does half of what I ask, I consider myself lucky."

Mom soon dragged me away from the throng and peppered me with questions. "Is that the doctor who examined your father? Has he had more dizzy spells? Why is he drinking alcohol? He *never* drinks. And why are we even at this party? Don't you guys have games to play tomorrow morning?"

"One game," I told her. "If our team gets four or five points, we can win this tournament, and a ten-thousand-dollar first prize. But Dad is gonna have to play his old enemy, and it's gonna be brutal."

She looked back at me like I was insane. "Your father doesn't have any enemies. He's an accountant."

"No," I told her. "You got that wrong. He's a great warrior—the chief of our tribe—and he needs to relax before he goes into battle."

We both glanced over at him. Dad had spilled green tea on his shirt and was dabbing at it with a napkin while adjusting his eyeglasses. "Morris?" she asked me dubiously.

"You'll see for yourself," I promised her.

"And what about you?" she asked. "In only two days . . . you seem very different."

"I'm the son of a warrior," I told her.

Angry as she still was, Mom smiled. "I like your new friend," she told me. "She has spunk."

Dad took the mic to sing an Elvis love song called "Love Me Tender," which he dedicated to my mom. "Ruth came all the way from New Jersey, by late-night transit bus, to check up on me. If that's not love, I don't know what is," he said. Then he crooned the syrupy song to Mom, and silly and off-key as it was, she smiled back at him. When it was done he came over and kissed her, and everyone clapped.

I was getting tired, and was on the point of telling Dad that we should go to sleep when Liu's mom and Mariel stepped up to the machine. They were the oddest pairing of the night—a rich blond society woman in a silk designer dress and diamonds, and a middle-class Chinese woman from the Bronx in jeans and a T-shirt, but they seemed to have struck a bond.

They sang "We Are Family"—finishing the final verse arm in arm, with badly synchronized leg kicks. They were taking their bows when, all of a sudden, a scream shrilled from one of the bedrooms.

The bedroom door flew open and Britney ran out, holding up her halter top to cover herself. The strap had been ripped. There was a red welt on her shoulder. "What happened, baby?" Mariel asked.

Britney took a quick breath and said, "Nothing. I'm okay, Mom. Let's go."

All eyes swung to Brad, who came strolling out of the bedroom, his hands in his pockets and a slight, uncomfortable smile on his handsome face.

Mariel stepped up to confront him. "What just happened in there?"

"Nothing," Brad said, and tried to walk past her.

But Mariel wasn't budging. "Her shirt is ripped and she's trying not to cry . . ."

"Wardrobe malfunction," he told her. "Ask her yourself."

Mariel turned and asked, "Brit?"

"It was nothing," Britney agreed in a whisper, turning her face away. "Mom, can we please just go now?"

Mr. Kinney had heard enough. "Why does that girl have a mark on her shoulder?" he demanded from his son.

Brad looked back at him. "Mind your own business."

Mr. Kinney reached out and grabbed Brad by the shirt. *"Don't you ever talk to me like that."*

Brad shoved him away. It didn't look like he pushed him that hard, but Mr. Kinney lost his footing and stumbled back and almost went down.

Brad looked a little surprised at how the situation was escalating. "Nothing happened," he repeated. "I'm getting out of here." And he took a step toward the door.

Mr. Kinney recovered and stepped in front of him. "You're not going anywhere."

Brad squared his shoulders. He was two inches taller than his dad and twenty years younger. "Don't you even think about putting your hands on me again," he warned.

I think they would have fought, and I believe youth might have won out and the swim captain might have decked the hedge fund king, but when the first blow fell, it came from an unexpected direction.

Mariel darted forward in a blur, drew back her right hand, and slapped Brad with her palm so that there was a very loud *thwacking* sound. He staggered back, tripped over a coffee table, and crashed to the floor. She stood over him. "Don't you *ever* touch my daughter again," she told him, and her face was so furious that Brad stayed down.

Then Mariel put her arm around Britney and quickly led her daughter out of the room.

My father came over to my mother, Kate, and me, and said, "Let's go, guys. This party's over."

26

A fearsome knight in armor was chasing me through the Loon Lake Academy, galloping after me on a warhorse. I hid in our chemistry lab, ran down the first-floor hallway, and burst into the library, but I couldn't shake him. He rode in right after me and drew his sword, and the fluorescent lights flickered off its sharp blade. Desperate, I crashed out through the library's window and fled along the stone path toward Grimwald Pond. Hoofbeats *click-clacked* behind me, gaining on me. I glanced back and the knight raised his visor. There was no face there—only two black holes for eyes—and then his sword flashed down . . .

And I woke up in my king-size bed in the Palace Royale Hotel, shaking and drenched in cold sweat. I hadn't had a nightmare that bad in years. I glanced at the roll-away cot next to my bed—Kate was snoring loudly. The clock on the night table read three a.m. and I was positive I wasn't going to be able to go back to sleep.

Click-clack. The hoofbeats from my nightmare came again, from our living room. I got up and tiptoed to the door in my bare feet and peered out. My father sat alone at the table in his blue cotton pajamas, moving chess pieces around a board with great concentration.

I quietly closed the bedroom door behind me and walked out into the living room. *Click*—Dad slammed down a bishop. *Clack*—he took a pawn. He sensed my presence and glanced up. "Touch of insomnia?"

"Bad dream," I said. "What's your excuse?"

"I never sleep before the final round," he told me. "But I'm guessing we'll both sleep well tomorrow night at home."

The circles under his eyes had deepened. He looked like an anxious old raccoon that had been flushed from its hiding place and was about to be run over by a tractor. "You look really terrible," I told him.

"Thanks. You look impressively rotten yourself," he said with a slight smile. "Let me guess—a weird nightmare?"

"Extremely weird. How did you know?"

"Chess nightmares," he chuckled. "Nothing quite like them. It's the stress of the tournament." Dad motioned to the chair across from him.

I sat and we looked at each other and both grinned at how ridiculous it was for us to be sitting there in a hotel suite in our pajamas at three a.m., facing each other across a chessboard. "So," he said, "looks like there will be only four Mind Cripplers tomorrow. I got a late-night text from Randolph. He took his son home. And they're not coming back."

I was surprised and a little angry. "But Mr. Kinney wanted to win the tournament more than any of us. We're so close to that ten thousand dollars now. Without them, we don't have a chance."

"He made a tough decision," Dad said, "but I think it was the right one. Sure, he set the whole thing up, from suites to team shirts. But he has to try to teach that bully a lesson . . ." My father broke off for a second, and then glanced up at me. "Anyway, we can still win first place," he pointed out. "We just need to sweep our last-round games."

"C'mon, Dad," I said. "There's no way I should even be two and two. Maybe lightning struck twice for once but never three times."

He gave a tired shrug. "I admit we're both in a little bit over our heads. But since we've come this far, we might as well keep trying to stay afloat."

I glanced down at the chess pieces. "What's this?"

"Just a game from a long time ago," he said. "I was white. George Liszt was black. We were playing for a spot on the junior national team that was going to compete in the world championships in Prague."

"And you remember the moves all these years later?"

"Some people remember song lyrics," Dad said. "Some can tell you the batting averages of every player in the Major Leagues. I remember chess games."

I looked down at the complicated position. "Did you win?"

"No," Dad said. "I was winning but the pressure got to me. And Liszt always knew just how to push me. He did this thing with his eyebrows, knitting them together. It drove me crazy. And he ground his teeth, but so softly that no tournament ref would call him on it. But I heard, and it totally screwed up my concentration. And during games he found insidious ways to remind me of my own worst faults and insecurities." Dad looked down at the pieces and shrugged. "He was also a pretty good chess player."

"He said you were better."

"Once upon a time," Dad admitted. "But that was way back when. What else did he say?"

I hesitated. "He told me about Nelson Stanwick."

Dad nodded, and I could see the regret in his eyes. "Yes, that was an awful thing," he said softly. "Nelson was a nice kid. Closest thing to a friend I had on the tournament circuit. Some mistakes you can't take back. You just have to find a way to live with them. What else?"

We were looking into each other's eyes. "He said you tried to hang yourself with your belt," I said softly.

My dad looked back at me and didn't say anything for several minutes. Then he whispered: "If you go rooting around in someone's closet, Daniel, you're going to find some shoddy old boots."

"Those are some pretty ragged old boots," I replied. And then: "Why?"

"I wanted . . . the pain to be over." As if to punctuate the thought, his hand swept across the chessboard, knocking over the pieces. When it came to rest on a fallen bishop I could see that it was trembling and making the chess piece shake. He sat there for a long time, not moving or speaking. Dad suddenly looked old and frail—like an eighty-year-old man in a fifty-year-old body. "That wasn't the first time I tried to kill myself at a chess tournament," he finally told me. "But it was the last."

"Unless that's what you're trying to do now," I whispered back. "We should just go home in the morning. We're not going to win this thing, and you look awful."

"*No,*" he said. "I'm staying to see it through. I've made my decision, and I told your mother last night that I won't go till it's over. And for what it's worth, I think you should at least try to win your last game."

"Of course I'll try, but . . ."

"Good," he said, "because you're better than you know. Now, there's something I want to show you." His hand swept over the chess pieces and, miraculously, they all seemed to leap to their starting positions. "This was the first game I ever memorized, when I was ten years old," he said. "It's a very silly game in a lot of ways, and it even has a silly name: 'A Night at the Opera.' It was played by Paul Morphy against two amateurs in 1858. He had been invited by one of them—a duke—to go to the opera and sit in his box. But when Morphy arrived, the duke challenged him to a game. Morphy wanted to see *The Marriage of Figaro*, but he agreed to play one game against the duke and a count who was also there. They played seventeen moves, and then Morphy checkmated them and watched the opera. It's just a trifle, but for sheer clarity it may be the best attacking game ever played in the history of chess. Now watch."

He made the first nine moves, throwing out occasional comments like "Philidor Defense" and "Fischer himself annotated this game," and then he stopped and looked at me. "Okay, up to now, any master might have made these moves. Now, watch this. Here comes Morphy. No one else could have done it. You can feel him through these moves . . . Go ahead, you make the moves. I'll tell you what to do . . ."

He told me to sacrifice my knight, and I did, and the next move he told me to sacrifice my bishop, and I did, and soon he was telling me to sacrifice my queen. As I moved the pieces I watched my dad, and listened to his voice, and tried to see what he was seeing and feel what he was feeling. I don't believe in séances or ghosts or spirit visitations, but something else—someone else—was right there with us in that room of the Palace Royale, floating above us, sitting next to me, staring down at the board and putting his hand over my hand as I moved the pieces, and smiling as if to say, "Don't you get it? It's a snap."

And I got it. Not all of it, but some of it. And when we were done with that game, Dad conjured the pieces back to their starting squares again and said, "Now, Morphy against his father, Alonzo. 1850. My favorite checkmate in the history of chess." So we played that one, too.

And at some point in the night my mother woke up and

came out, but she didn't say a word to break the spell. She just stood there watching and listening, trying to figure out what was going on as my father told me: "Fischer against Donald Byrne, the Game of the Century. 1956. He was only thirteen years old. Grunfeld Defense: Three Knights Variation. Hungarian Attack. Now, you move the pieces, Daniel . . . and let's go!"

27

I walked into the Palace Royale's pool fifteen minutes after it opened, and Britney was the only one there, swimming slow, sad laps like a mermaid in mourning. She wasn't wearing her teensy-weensy purple bikini, but rather a sea-green one-piece that covered much more of her. The welt on her shoulder was almost gone, I noticed.

I stood for a few seconds near the door, watching her circle back and forth, and she looked almost achingly beautiful. When she reached the wall she did a slow turn, saw me, and stopped. "Hi, Daniel," she said. "I was hoping you'd come for a morning swim."

"More like a morning sink," I told her, wading down the steps and doing a few splashy dog-paddle strokes.

"If anyone's sinking here, it's probably me," Britney replied in a soft voice.

I waded over to her. The Palace Royale Hotel had comfortable beds, but I was beginning to think that nobody got much sleep in them. Britney looked tired and sad—as if she had been reliving last night's fight with Brad over and over for hours. "I thought maybe you went home last night," I said.

"It was so late that we thought we might as well stay," she told me. "But we're going as soon as my mom wakes up." She gazed down at the smooth surface of the pool. "It wasn't a great night."

"Yeah . . ." I hesitated.

"But it was probably a good thing that it happened," she whispered. "Now I'm free."

"Free from what?"

"Brad and I split up last night," Britney said. "I told him I wanted to break up and we got into a huge fight and all of a sudden he just grabbed me. I think the reason he lost control is that he was so angry at me."

"No excuse . . ."

"No, it sure isn't," she agreed in a low voice. She climbed out of the pool and sat down on the side with her legs dangling in the water. I stood awkwardly in front of her. She was silent and motionless beneath the fluorescent lights, and tiny droplets of water fell from her hair and ran down her shoulders. When she finally spoke, her voice was soft and fragile. "I was really afraid. He had this crazy look in his eyes."

I was trying so hard to figure out how to say the right thing I probably had a crazy look in my eyes, too. "I guess it's over now," I said at last.

"Yes," she said. "For sure it's over. Come sit next to me for a minute."

I pulled myself out of the pool and sat next to her on the side. We were alone in the large room. There were yellow tiles on the walls and the ceiling was painted white and had several long cracks. She turned and looked at me and said, "I broke up with him because of you."

"What?" I must have looked really freaked out because Britney smiled.

"Don't look so scared," she said. "I'm not after you, lover boy. But you're such an amazingly nice guy. Spending time with you—and watching you and Liu—has helped me realize that I picked Brad for the wrong reasons. Like, he's a senior. And he's so superconfident."

"A champion," I added. "Handsome. Brilliant."

"None of that really matters. I think maybe it was because of my dad leaving us. It felt safe . . . to have a boyfriend who was older and always in control. Anyway, you and Liu are so cute together, you just seem to be . . . having so much fun . . . and you're not trying to control her or tell her what to do . . . I knew I had to get away from him. So thank you." She leaned over and kissed me on the cheek. It was the second time in my life—and in the last twenty-four hours—that a girl had kissed me.

I looked into her beautiful blue eyes and I didn't know what to say, so I mumbled, "Anytime."

Britney giggled. "You're blushing."

"Am I? Listen, I better get back up to the room. We have our final round soon and . . . without Brad and his father—" I broke off.

"What happened to them?" she asked.

"Mr. Kinney took Brad home last night," I told her. "I have a feeling it's not too pleasant in their house right now."

She nodded and gazed down into the water. "It shouldn't be." Then she looked back at me. "But you guys are still playing the last round? You're gonna finish it out?"

"We'll take a shot. But we have to win all our games. That will never happen."

"Maybe not," she said, "but what I told you when we were standing in that pond still holds. I think you're better than you know. Good luck, Daniel."

I got up and headed away to check on my father and left her sitting on the edge of the pool alone.

28

We held the last team meeting of the Mind Cripplers in our suite, with my mom and sister looking on as mystified observers. "They posted the standings and the final pairings early this morning," Eric told us. "We're tied for first in the team championship with the Scarsdale Savants, captained by George Liszt." Eric turned to my father. "You two are playing on board one in the final round. Even though we're short a player, if you beat him and all the rest of us win our games, we'll top them on a head-to-head tiebreaker and win first place and the ten grand!"

"Ten thousand dollars?" my mother whispered. "Really, Morris?"

"I'm using my share to buy an iPad," Kate announced.

"You don't have a share," I pointed out. "You've done nothing. Except be a distraction."

"My part of the family share will be more than five hun-

dred dollars," Kate informed me. "And I haven't done nothing. I sang four songs last night. Now, show me the green!"

"First we have to beat the Savants," Dr. Chisolm cautioned.
"And none of us have easy games. Your father is playing a top
grandmaster."

Dad hadn't slept or eaten or shaved in two days and nights,
and he looked beyond run-down—like one of the last two cars
weaving around a track at a demolition derby, its doors and
wheels and engine hanging together by only a couple of last
stubborn screws. "Fitting that it comes down to us," he said
softly. "The two old gunfighters across the board from each
other at high noon. No big surprise, really."

"I guess the only surprise is that board one won't actually
be in the tournament hall," Eric told him. "The organizers
have heard stories of the history of bad blood between you
two, so they're not taking any chances. They're moving you
guys to a secret private playing area they've prepared just for
the championship game."

This seemed to bother Dad, as if the prospect of being split
off from the rest of us and locked in a secret room with George
Liszt wasn't his idea of the best way to spend a Sunday morning. "That's highly unusual," he muttered. "Where are they
moving us?"

"No one knows for sure," Eric admitted. "I heard a rumor
that they've rented the hotel's penthouse because it's quiet and
full of light. At least you'll be comfortable. Anyway, it'll be just
the two of you and a referee, and a couple of closed-circuit

cameras filming the action so that we can all watch and cheer you on from downstairs."

"I wonder who came up with that idea?" Dad muttered.

Mom heard the unease and suspicion in his tone and looked concerned. "I don't understand, Morris. Why won't you be playing with everyone else?"

"Special players merit special treatment, Ruth," he told her with an ironic smile. "I hope they don't forget the padded walls and the straitjackets." Dad paused and pressed his fingers together thoughtfully. "George is probably behind this penthouse notion. He knows I don't like to feel isolated and that too much glare distracts me. He's already starting to screw with me." He turned to Eric. "Okay, what about the rest of you?"

"My dad's playing an international master named Schmidt," Eric said. "He came all the way from Munich for this tournament. He's gonna be real tough."

"I'll send him back to Germany with some unpleasant memories," Dr. Chisolm promised, but I could see he was worried. International masters are world-class players—one step below grandmasters.

"I've drawn a master from Cincinnati named Vanderkoen," Eric told us. "He's got his own Web site on opening traps, so I'd better bring a land mine detector."

"What about me?" I asked.

Eric's eyes swung in my directon. "Roger Moffatt. He's kind of a celebrity—I've seen him written up in magazines. He's a software billionaire who's pledged to use computers to solve chess in the next ten years. In the meantime, he's trying to make the master rank. He's hired some of the best players in Russia and America to tutor him, and he's been climbing toward master for three or four years. Now he's a top expert, right on the edge of getting it. So we all have our work cut out for us." Eric paused, and then added: "But if we all somehow win, then we win it all."

My father glanced at his watch. "Team prayer," he said, and my mom shot him a curious look. But a team tradition is a team tradition, and a moment later we were on our knees, holding hands. "Ruth, Kate, please join us," Dad invited.

They both hesitated and then got down next to us. I reached for Kate's hand. "Did you wash that recently?" she demanded.

"Do you want your share of the prize money?" Dad asked her sternly.

Kate took my right hand. My left was already holding Eric's right. My father said: "Dr. Chisolm, I believe it's your turn to deliver the team prayer."

Dr. Chisolm looked around at us and nodded. "Bow your heads," he said, and we did. "Moment of silence," he intoned, and we were all quiet. I hadn't said a prayer during the whole tournament, but now I silently asked God to protect my father during this last round.

Dr. Chisolm looked serious, as if he were pondering what this last round meant and choosing his words very carefully. "Lord," he finally said, "this is the last round and the Mind Cripplers are really up against it. We need your help and guidance. A surgeon probably shouldn't admit this, but I feel a little like when I'm heading into an operation that I know will be extremely difficult. On one hand I'm confident I'll perform well and do everything that can possibly be done, but I also know the margin between success and failure in such cases can sometimes be so tiny . . . so fragile . . . even so unfair . . ."

He broke off for a second and looked across the circle at me. "But far more important things have happened here than just chess. Watching what a son will do for his father has touched me and taught me." His eyes moved from me to his own son and he kept going. For a moment it was hard to say if he was talking to us or to himself.

"Sometimes, we want the best for our kids, and we push too hard. We keep aloof from them or we pressure them too much, we hide from them or we grab them with both arms. Either way we run the risk of pushing them out the door, of teaching them the wrong lessons, and of turning them into men we wouldn't want them to be." My father nodded very slightly.

"In our first team prayer," Dr. Chisolm noted, "Grandmaster Pratzer said that the great blessing of this tournament was that we were able to have this time together. I've come to see the wisdom in his words. So instead of asking you for something, Lord, let me close this prayer by just saying thank you"—his usually confident voice broke, but he managed to finish—"for helping us to realize how lucky we are to have such fine sons. Amen."

"Amen," we said around the circle.

I saw Eric looking back at his father, and for a few moments there was a tenderness in his usually intense black eyes.

Then we were all standing and trooping out of the suite toward the elevators and the playing hall below. I noticed that my mother walked along with us and stayed very near my father, as if keeping a nervous eye on him. He was grim-faced and silent.

When we were riding down in the elevator, he put his hand on my shoulder and advised me in a low voice: "Don't be intimidated. Software billionaires put on their pants one leg at a time like the rest of us."

"I'm not sure exactly what that means," I said.

"It means that chess is mental combat between two and only two people," he told me. "When Bobby Fischer took the title from Spassky, all the grandmasters in Russia couldn't help him. Once the clock starts it will just be the two of you. Play one strong move after another and you'll do fine. Any man who thinks he's going to solve chess deserves to be taken down a peg."

"Thanks," I told him. We were nearing the second floor. "For what it's worth," I whispered, "I think that deep down George Liszt is scared of you."

The elevator *pinged* at the second floor and the doors started to open. My dad shot me what was meant to be a confident wink, but he was now so tense the twitching of his eye made it look like his cheeks might shatter.

We stepped out of the elevator and a man in a suit with a TOURNAMENT OFFICIAL badge immediately hurried up to my father and said, "Grandmaster Pratzer? It's an honor, sir. Right this way, please. A private elevator is waiting . . ."

My mother grabbed my father's arm and said his name.

He gave her a tense smile back and said, "Don't worry, Ruth, everything will be fine," turned, and followed the tournament official to a small private elevator that was waiting for them. He faced out at me as the doors closed, our eyes met one last time, and then he was gone.

Moffatt was a short man in his late thirties with a nose like a hawk's beak and the bossy manners of someone who's used to being obeyed by everyone around him. He wasn't dressed extravagantly—just black jeans and a nice button-down striped shirt—but his entourage was very intimidating.

When I got to our table, he was already seated, surrounded by his people. An intense Indian assistant who didn't seem to know or care about chess stood near him listening to two cell phones at the same time and giving Moffatt a running report on some kind of business deal. The assistant glowered at me, as if to ask: "Don't you realize my business with my boss is a lot more important than your stupid chess game?"

A solidly built middle-aged woman wearing a brightly colored kerchief stood behind my opponent, giving him a neck and shoulder massage and urging him to relax. On Moffatt's right side, a man with graying hair, who I guessed was a high-priced chess tutor, whispered some last-minute chess advice in Russian-accented English, moving the pieces around the board at lightning speed to demonstrate his points.

"Daniel Pratzer? Sit down. That's your chair," Moffatt said when I walked up, holding out his hand and motioning me to the seat opposite him, as if I was late for a business interview but he was willing to give me the benefit of the doubt. "You've had quite a tournament, haven't you? And your father—my God, I saw his last game against Sanchez. A gem, wasn't it, Fyodor?" The Russian chess tutor didn't say anything but his bushy eyebrows rose as if in grudging salute. "Sit, fill out your score sheet. I have something I need to attend to," Moffatt said, and then he started talking to his assistant about buying an imaging company while I tried to find a pencil with a good point.

The final round began a few minutes late, so once they banished all nonplayers from the tournament hall Moffatt and I had a brief time to chat. "What exactly does it mean to 'solve' chess?" I asked him.

He looked pleased that I had heard of him and his work. "All games can be solved," he told me. "Checkers was solved—we know the optimal order of moves that will generate a successful result every time, and the correct responses to deviations. Chess is far more complicated than checkers, but in the next ten or fifteen years we should have it licked."

"Won't that kill the game?" I asked him.

He shrugged. "If it does, it does. My passion is solving puzzles. Then I move on to the next challenge."

I looked back at him. This little man was dismissing with a careless shrug the potential responsibility for ruining an ancient and beautiful game that had given pleasure to millions. The chess gods my father had conjured up in our hotel suite the night before weren't going to put up with this. I looked back at Moffatt—at the smirk on his controlling face—and I surprised myself by saying in a low voice: "I'm going to beat you."

For a moment he appeared thrown by this, and then his gray eyes swirled angrily and he said, "No you're not. I'm just a few points away from becoming a master. Do you have any idea of the time and expense it's taken to achieve this? If I lose to a beginner like you, I'll shed hundreds of rating points. That's not going to happen."

A loud buzzer sounded at the front of the hall, and a man with a microphone walked out onto the dais. "On behalf of the organizers, I'd like to thank you all for playing in our tournament. Before we begin the final round, Former World Champion Contender Arkady Shuvalovitch will say a few final words. Arkady?" He paused and looked around. "Has anyone seen Arkady?"

There were several awkward seconds. Then a heavily accented voice rang out: "Yes, I am here!" The schlubby-looking man who had opened the tournament reappeared in what I think was the same ill-fitting suit. He ran forward from the wings, took the microphone, and—in his eagerness—tripped and fell off the dais. He got up, dusted himself off, and looked out at us. "Fathers, sons, mothers, daughters, thank you for playing so well and trying so hard. Always remember, chess is like a camel. It is burdened with a hump, but that also keeps it alive in the middle of the desert. Good luck to you all."

He walked off the stage as a voice boomed over the PA system: "START YOUR CLOCKS."

30

The final round of a chess tournament, I discovered, has its own grim intensity, as players who have labored long and hard collect themselves for one last surge. At the front of the hall, the contenders know they're close to prize money, trophies, and rating points but that a loss now will turn triumph into tragedy. In the middle, strong players who have made a few mistakes and dropped a game or two sit down with tight, combative faces, determined to win their last one and salvage a decent result. At the back of the hall, weaker players who have struggled and lost many games tap their last reserves of stamina and self-respect to try to avoid a complete debacle.

I was in the exact middle of the hall, surrounded by strong players who had won as many games as they had lost and were intent on finishing with a victory. I could feel their concentration surging around me, a silent electrical buzz that crackled in the air.

I had the black pieces against Moffatt, and when he slammed his king pawn down and stared across at me, I was surprised to find that I wasn't at all nervous. Opening jitters had unsettled me throughout the tournament, but in this final round my mind remained crystal clear.

I looked back at Moffatt and mentally stripped away all the sports cars and chess tutors and zeroes in his bank account. Tonight he would no doubt go back to a penthouse apartment in some supertrendy neighborhood of Manhattan, while I would drive back through the Lincoln Tunnel to our three-bedroom house with the busted garage door and the leaky toilet, but right now it was just the two of us at the table— two brains locked in mental combat.

I remembered my dad's advice: "If you're up against a strong player, get him off the book and make him think for himself." I played Alekhine's Defense, which my father had told me about. "Alexander Alekhine, who defeated the great Capablanca to become world champion, introduced it in 1921," Dad had explained. "It's not played much because it looks so ugly for black at the beginning. But if black plays the first few moves correctly, it leads to an open position with good attacking chances."

At first Moffatt seemed confident. His white pawns pushed my knight around and took over the center. Soon he was castled safely and had a formidable pawn wall, while my black pieces looked underdeveloped. But my father had counseled me to be patient. "Just play one sound move after another and chip away at white's center pawns, and his position will start to crumble."

Moffatt didn't panic—his tutors had prepared him well. But as the game went on and I castled my own king and started to undermine his center pawn mass, he looked a little irritated. I was rated nearly nine hundred points lower than him. I could tell that he already thought of himself as a master, and me as a rank beginner, and he was putting all kinds of pressure on himself to crush me.

One strong move at a time, my dad had said. I flashed back to the previous night, when my father had replayed his favorite games from memory and Fischer and Morphy had come alive and hovered above me, whispering their most basic lessons into my head. "Get your king to safety. Control the center of the board. Develop your pieces to useful squares— knights first, then bishops, and then rooks. Keep your pawns connected and they'll fight harder for you, like comrades who can cheer one another on."

I didn't try to do anything fancy—I just made sure that every one of my moves had a logical point behind it. Moffatt's irritation turned to annoyance and then anger. He bit his lip and rubbed the sides of his chin with his palms. "Where the hell are you getting these moves from?" he hissed as we reached the middle game on fairly even turns and I started to switch from defending to attacking. "You're just a class D player, for God's sake!"

I thought to myself, This is a part of who I am that I never knew before, part of my birthright. My father wasn't a great swimmer or runner or football player, but he had one of the greatest chess brains of his generation. And maybe he'd passed a little bit of it on to me. So maybe I'd never be the best athlete or the most popular kid at the Loon Lake Academy, but I suddenly felt like I could take apart this bossy, boastful billionaire.

I didn't say any of that out loud, though. What I did say was: "Please be quiet, or I'll have to call over a ref," and then I made my strongest move yet and got up from the table. I had learned that when my opponent starts getting frustrated, it infuriates him or her even more to stare across at an empty chair. I decided to let Moffatt stew alone for a few minutes while I checked on my dad.

There was already a crowd in the common area, watching the two large monitors. I could see and hear my father, and he didn't look good. He was breathing in gasps, his face was pale, and tiny beads of sweat threaded together across his forehead. George Liszt had the white pieces and was attacking mercilessly. Every time Dad tried to wiggle out of pressure, Liszt responded immediately, as if he had foreseen my father's move and had the answer ready.

My mother spotted me and hurried over, with Kate trailing behind. "Your father's in trouble," Mom said, and since she didn't know anything about chess I figured she was worried about the way he looked. "Daniel, we've got to get him out."

"It's his last game and he's already in the middle of it," I told her. "He'll be done soon."

"Just look at his face," she whispered. "He looks like he's melting."

"That monster is going to crush him," Kate added, for once not sarcastic but actually sounding worried herself.

On the monitor Liszt did look like a monster—he appeared twice as big as my dad. It was like watching Godzilla playing chess with the next person he was planning to devour. Liszt sat hunched forward in an aggressive and intimidating pose, as if he might slip forward at any moment and crush my dad to smithereens. His thick arms rested on either side of the table like two anacondas, and he aimed his fierce laser stare right between my father's eyes, as if trying to melt down the front of Dad's skull. The big man's jaw, beneath his thick black beard, sawed very slightly back and forth.

"Ask him to stop grinding his teeth," my father demanded to the tournament ref, who sat off-screen.

"I'm sorry, but I don't hear anything," the ref answered.

Dad looked directly at Liszt. "Why don't you cut it out and just play chess?"

"I am playing, Morris," Liszt responded in a mocking rumble. "Keep calm. You don't want to get upset, do you? We know what happens when you get upset."

"*Silence, both of you,*" the tournament ref commanded, and the game resumed.

I had to go back to my own game, so I gave Mom a reassuring hug. "I'll be back soon," I promised her. "Don't worry about Dad. He'll get through this okay."

I don't think she heard me. She was staring at the monitor screen, where my father's right hand had drifted to his left wrist to take his pulse. As I headed back into the tournament hall I heard her whisper, "Morris, please . . . calm down."

31

Moffatt had already moved when I returned, and my side of the chess clock was running. He was sitting with his arms crossed, staring at the board and glancing at the flashing digital display of the minutes I had left, as if hoping that I would take too long to come back and lose on time. He looked disappointed to see me walk up. I gave him a little smile, as if to say, "Did you really think I would hand you this game?"; slipped back into my chair; and saw right away that he had overreached.

My dad had counseled me to ignore the higher ratings of opponents and just play the best chess I could. Now I understood that his warning cut both ways. Because of my low rating, Moffatt saw me as a class D player, and he apparently couldn't get that out of his head. He was being wildly overaggressive and trying for a quick mate.

I made a sound defensive move, but instead of backing off he pressed his attack. Three or four moves later it was clear that he wasn't going to be able to checkmate me, and that he had badly compromised his position. Not only had his attack faltered, but he had left himself open to a counterattack. I stopped defending and started firing off aggressive salvos of my own, and the billionaire panicked.

He took longer to move, and kept glancing across at me, waiting for me to make the beginner's blunder he was certain was coming. But I was scenting blood, and I wasn't about to slip up. I sacrificed a pawn for open lines and ripped his king's position apart. Finally, Moffatt saw that the end was near. Fear gleamed in his eyes, and then grudging acceptance— he was going to lose this game in a few more moves and there was no escape.

The chess player in him stepped back, and the hard-driving businessman took over. "Listen to me, Pratzer," Moffatt whispered, leaning forward and speaking in such a low voice that only I could hear it. "If I drop this game, all the time and work and money I've sunk into making master go out the window. There is a way for us to reach an . . . accommodation . . . where I get what I want . . . and richly deserve . . . and you get *substantial* restitution—" He broke off and raised his eyebrows as if to assure me that if I let him win, the payoff would be well worth my while.

I looked back at him coldly, seeing him now for the scoundrel that he was. "If you talk to me again, I'll call over the ref, and report what you just offered. Maybe you'll solve chess one day, but you're going to lose this game and you don't deserve to be a master." I reached down and made a killer move. "Check."

Three moves later, Moffatt gave up gracelessly. He stared back at me with narrowed eyes and cobralike fury, as if I had upended all his carefully laid plans and he wanted to sink his fangs into me, and knocked over his king. "What a waste," he hissed. "What a damn shame."

But I had finished with him and was already moving to hand in my score sheet and check on my father. I ran into Eric, who had also just finished. "How'd it go?" he asked.

"Busted the billionaire!" I reported. "And you?"

"Mind-crippled the master!" he exulted. "And my dad is winning, too. The German international master must still be jet-lagged. So we have a real chance to win first prize, if your father can pull his game out."

"That's a big if," I told him as we hurried out the door of the tournament hall. More than two hundred people had gathered in front of the two monitors to watch my dad and Liszt duke it out. A master stood on a podium, commentating. As we walked up I heard him say: "Black is not lost yet, but he's sure not look-ing good." Liu spotted me and hurried over. "Your father's coming apart at the seams," she told me. "He's taken two bath-room breaks in the last fifteen minutes to try to pull himself together. He's also losing badly on time. Your mom can't even watch. Whatever Liszt is doing is making your dad crazy."

On the monitor, my father looked like he might have a nervous breakdown at any moment. He was trembling and drenched in sweat, as if he had just stepped out of a sauna. His arms were not folded in front of him in his usual position, but rather they were clutching the sides of the table as if he were dizzy and bracing himself. When he squinted down at the board he looked like his head was spinning, and when he glanced up at Liszt he looked like a torture victim staring into the eyes of his tormentor.

Mom and Kate were sitting on chairs near a window, by themselves. Every few seconds my mother would turn to the screen and glance at her husband and then quickly look away. I walked over to her, and Liu and Eric followed. "Hey, Mom . . ."

I was going to tell her that I had won my game, but when she turned her head to look at me I could see at once that she didn't care about chess results. Deep lines of worry crosshatched her face. She grabbed my wrist and I could feel her desperation. "Daniel," she said. Just my name. But I understood it was an urgent plea.

"It's almost over," I told her. "They're moving into the end-game."

She shook her head. "Now," she said.

"I don't know where they are, Mom," I told her.

Suddenly the crowd reacted. I glanced at the monitor and saw that my father had made a move.

"That's a fascinating move for black," the master said. "On its face it doesn't look sound, but it's certainly interesting. I admit I didn't see it coming. I'll have to take a few seconds and study it."

Liszt clearly didn't think it was sound. The big grandmaster caught my father's eye, smiled, made a quick move of his own in reply, and then slid his thumb and index finger over his throat and around the front of his neck.

"He's telling your father that he's choking," Eric surmised.

"No," I said, "he's reminding my dad of something a lot worse."

"What's worse than choking away the final game?" Eric asked.

"Stanwick," I whispered.

"Who's Stanwick?" my mom demanded.

Just then Dr. Chisolm hurried over to join us.

"Hey, Dad, did you win?" Eric asked.

Dr. Chisolm nodded, but he was staring at my father on the monitor. "I'm not sure I like the way he's rubbing his jaw," he muttered.

"His jaw?" Kate asked. "Dad has lousy teeth so . . ."

"And his left shoulder," Dr. Chisolm noted.

I could see on the monitor that Dad's hand had slid down from rubbing his jaw to massaging his left shoulder.

Dr. Chisolm dug out his cell phone. "It could be nothing," he said, "but . . ."

I realized that the heart is on the left side of the body, and guessed that tightness in the jaw and pain in the left shoulder are warning signs of serious heart trouble. "Who are you calling?" I asked.

"I got the cell phone number of one of the high tournament officials," Dr. Chisolm said. "Just in case."

On the monitor, Liszt did something really strange. He

had taken off his belt, and now he brought the leather strap up to his neck and let the ends hang down from his shoulders.

"What the heck is that guy doing?" Eric asked.

Dr. Chisolm punched buttons on his cell phone. "No answer. I'll try again."

"Please put that belt back on and stop misbehaving," the tournament ref rebuked Liszt.

But it was too late. The sight of the belt, and no doubt the reminder it was, unhinged my father. For a moment I thought he was going to go over the table at Liszt. Then he muttered a curse, got up from the table, and bolted.

A second later, Dr. Chisolm got through. He spoke a few quick words and then turned to us, the cell phone still pressed to the side of his face. "Your father left the playing room, and before they could stop him he ran out of the penthouse suite," he told me.

"Where is he?" my mother asked.

"No one knows," Dr. Chisolm told her. "He's gone."

32

"They've checked the penthouse floor and they can't find him," Dr. Chisolm reported to my mom. "Hotel security thinks he's still inside the hotel. There are doormen at all exits, and none of them recall seeing him walking out. Do you think he might have gone to your room to look for you?"

Mom nodded hopefully and hurried off toward the elevators with Kate trailing a step behind. Dr. Chisolm ran to join them, and Eric followed.

"Don't you want to go?" Liu asked me.

"If he's in our suite, they'll find him," I told her. "But I don't think he is."

She heard a note of fear in my voice. "Where do you think he is, Daniel?"

I recalled what Grandmaster Liszt had told me about what my dad had done long ago when he cracked under extreme pressure. "I think he might be up on the roof."

Liu looked back at me. "Why the roof?"

"Once, at a tournament in San Francisco, the police had to wrestle him off a hotel roof," I told her in a low voice. "And it happened at a couple of other tournaments, too, when he came unglued. And he was playing Liszt up in the penthouse, so the roof is very close."

"Let's go," she said.

We ran to the elevators and were soon rocketing up to the thirty-fifth floor. "There's no button for the penthouse floor," I pointed out, "let alone for the roof. They're probably both locked off."

"It's a hotel, not a prison," Liu said. "We'll find a way."

We reached the thirty-fifth floor, bolted down the hallway, and found a flight of stairs heading up. I took them three at a time, with Liu right behind me. The next stairwell had a *P* instead of a floor number. A closed door said: PENT-HOUSE FLOOR. PRIVATE.

"Want to take a quick look?" Liu asked.

"Let's keep going," I told her.

We climbed a narrow metal staircase that corkscrewed upward into semidarkness. I imagined Dad circling up these stairs alone, trembling, needing light and air, and craving escape from the pressure he felt closing in on all sides of him.

At the top of the metal stairs was a heavy steel door. In the dim lighting, I could just read the red sign on it: WARNING: EMERGENCY DOOR. KEEP CLOSED BY NEW YORK STATE LAW. ALARMS WILL SOUND.

"Does this qualify as an emergency?" I asked Liu.

"Definitely," she said, and pushed the handle of the door. It stayed shut.

I raised my foot and kicked the handle hard, and the door burst open. No alarms sounded. Either the sign was a bluff or the system wasn't working. I stepped through the doorway and Liu followed me out into blinding sunlight.

New York is a jungle of skyscrapers and we stepped out onto the roof—the sun-splashed uppermost tier. The tops of other skyscrapers were all around us, with spires and cell phone towers. Far below, Broadway looked as narrow as a bowling alley, the cars and buses were nickels and dimes, and the people crawled like beetles.

There was nothing up there—no furniture, no ladders or construction material, not even a bench. I guess they were afraid a strong wind might blow debris off the flat surface and onto the heads of pedestrians far below. I looked in every direction and didn't spot my father. "There," Liu suddenly said. "Oh my God."

Dad was standing at the very edge of a corner of the roof, his back to us, looking down at the street below. We ran toward him, and with each step I dreaded that he would slip off and suddenly disappear right before our eyes. When we got close, Liu hung back. "You talk to him alone, Daniel."

I stepped toward him, but didn't have a clue what to say. "Hey, Dad, I thought I might find you up here," I said, knowing how ridiculous it sounded.

He was facing south, looking down at lower Manhattan all the way to the Statue of Liberty raising her torch above New York Harbor. He didn't turn his head at the sound of my voice. I wasn't sure he even heard me.

"How are you doing?" I asked.

Long seconds dragged by. "Not too well," he finally answered. And then, softly, "I'm sorry, Daniel." I thought he might be turning to face me, but instead he pitched forward into nothingness.

33

I didn't have time to think or feel afraid—I just stepped forward and caught him by the arm, and held on to him. We stood clinging together, at the edge of the roof above the great city that swept beneath and away in all directions. Dad was trembling so badly that I was afraid he might shake us both over the lip at any second.

Behind me, I heard Liu shouting out my name, and begging us to be careful. "Easy does it," I said.

"I wasn't trying to jump. I'm just feeling a little dizzy," Dad whispered back.

"Then let's sit down," I suggested. "Because I'm not letting go. If you go over the edge, I'm going, too."

"Okay, let's sit," he agreed.

Slowly, holding on to each other, we sat down side by side on the edge of the roof, with our legs hanging over the side of the building. I felt a bit dizzy myself, so I kept my eyes fixed on Lady Liberty's torch and tried to figure out what to say. "Mom is downstairs waiting for us," I told him very gently. "You have nothing more to prove here. Not to me, not to George Liszt, not even to Fischer and Morphy. I've seen you at your best—I'll never forget what you did to Grandmaster Sanchez. It's enough."

"No, it's not enough," he replied in a whisper. "I wasn't going to jump just now . . . but part of me wanted to."

I let go of his arm and took his right hand. It felt cold and clammy. "What are you talking about?"

"George Liszt has led the life I should have had," he whispered. "He's traveled to international tournaments, and won brilliancy prizes, and followed his stars. Not a week has gone by in my tiny office in New Jersey when, on some deep level, I haven't thought of who I should have been, and rued the day I quit, and hated myself for the weak coward I am. I pushed it far away and tried to pretend it wasn't there, but this tournament—and especially this last game—has forced me to dredge it up and face it. You want to hear the truth about Grandmaster Pratzer? That's who your father is. A man who regrets his life."

"You walked away from this crazy chess world for good reasons."

"That's what I tried to tell myself," he agreed. "And it's true enough on some level. But it's also a big lie."

I held his hand tightly. "There are two sides to everything. You made a mature decision."

"I don't know," he admitted. "I love you and your sister and your mom, and I want to go home. But I also know this—I see it very clearly. There's a big part of me that can't possibly leave now. I can't walk back into my office on Monday morning and pretend this never happened, and pick up the first tax forms on my desk and sip the bitter coffee from the cracked mug."

"What's the alternative?" I asked him.

A spark seemed to kindle in his black eyes, and he squeezed my hand. "There's only one thing to do. I need to go down there and face Liszt and finish this game. Not for your mother, or for you, or for anyone else in the world. This is something I need to do for me. *For me.* And I'm ready."

I spoke softly. "I'm not sure you can handle it. You look terrible, and I'm worried about your heart. Also, they probably disqualified you as soon as you left the penthouse. Anyway, you're almost surely out of time by now."

"Got to do it," he whispered, and the spark in his eye had kindled into a flame. It danced and flickered like a kind of madness, but it also gave him new strength and determination. "Got to try. You're my son. Help me."

I took a deep breath. "Okay, Dad. I'll stay with you every step of the way. And the first one's going to be the hardest. Can we slide back on our butts and get away from the edge before we stand up?"

Dad's sweaty body trembled. "I don't know if I can move," he said. "I'm kind of frozen here."

"Just a few inches," I encouraged. "Backward. Come on. One, two . . . three."

We slid inch by inch back from the abyss, and then stood up and started walking across the roof.

Liu hurried over. "Hi, Mr. Pratzer. Can I help you?"

"Take my other arm," he said. "I'm feeling better now, but I'm still a little dizzy."

Liu took his other arm and we braced him between us and led him back toward the stairs. "Let's go quickly," Dad said. "I can't have much time left on my clock."

"Don't worry about the game," Liu told him. "It really doesn't matter."

"It matters to my father," I told her. "He's going to go down and finish. And that's his decision, so we have to respect it and help him."

Liu looked back at me. "Great," she muttered, "two insane men in one family. I really know how to pick 'em."

"I like this girl, Daniel," my father told me as we took another step. "You might want to keep her around for a while."

34

"It's over," George Liszt shouted as soon as he saw us walk into the penthouse playing area. "He's disqualified himself. Who knows where he's been?"

The ref called over the tournament director, a well-dressed, dignified older man, who ordered that Dad's clock be stopped while the whole mess was sorted out. I saw that Dad only had four minutes and seven seconds remaining.

"I know where he's been," I told them. "On the roof. By himself. There's a surveillance camera up there if you need proof." I made that up, but it sounded plausible.

Liszt turned to the tournament director. "He could have had help. He could have checked the position on a computer. He could have made a cell phone call to anyone."

Dad stayed silent, so I jumped to his defense. "My dad doesn't have a cell phone with him," I said. "And he didn't bring a computer on this trip. He just needed a breath of fresh air. You know what I think?"

Liszt glared at me. "I couldn't care less."

"I think you don't have the guts to face him and finish this," I said. "I think you're a bully, and you did your best to scare me into taking him home, but right now you're the one who's scared."

The enormous grandmaster stepped toward me threateningly, but my father cut him off and said softly: "George, my son has a point. Why don't we just sit down at the board and finish this ourselves?"

Liszt looked at my father and saw something he didn't like. Despite my dad's paleness, despite the fact that he was sweaty and still trembling, there was a new resolve in his face and a competitive fire glowing in his eyes. "No," Liszt growled. "I'm out of here. It's over."

The tournament director glanced from Liszt to my dad, sizing the situation up. "One question—why *did* you leave the playing area, Grandmaster Pratzer?"

I realized that the cameras were rolling and that whatever Dad answered would be heard and seen by hundreds of people downstairs. "Because I'm a coward sometimes, and I was afraid, and I couldn't handle the pressure," Dad said softly, looking into the eyes of the tournament director. Then Dad's voice hardened. "But I can handle it now."

"Now is too late, you wacko," George Liszt told him. "It's over. I've won and I'm leaving. Give me my money."

"*It's not over,*" the tournament director declared with authority. "We're outside the rule book here. This is my call, and

I declare the game on. It's black's move." He looked at Liu and me. "Only the two players can stay."

"Goodbye," I said to my father.

He whispered, "Thanks, Daniel. Tell Mom I love her," and sat down at the chessboard. "George," he said, "we've had this coming a long time. I believe it's my move."

Liu and I rode down in the elevator. "Wow," she said, "that was intense. Do you think he can really win the game in four minutes? Or maybe it doesn't matter whether he wins or loses. Maybe he just needs to finish."

"It matters," I told her.

The doors opened, and we found ourselves in the crowded common area, where the excitement had reached a fever pitch. My father had taken forty precious seconds to think about his move, and the master was on his podium, waving his arms as he moved pieces on a demo board.

"Grandmaster Pratzer is offering to sacrifice a knight for two pawns," the master explained. "It looks to me to be a highly speculative sacrifice, but he must have calculated that if white grabs the knight he will have a hard time stopping black's pawns from advancing."

George Liszt spent ten minutes staring hard at the board, pondering that same calculation. He looked like a man at a fork in a road, trying to pick a route and suspecting that either path might lead to disaster. He leaned forward and tilted back, he crossed his arms and laid them flat, he squinted at the board and then he glared across at my father. Dad gave him a slightly amused smile back, as if to say: "So you see it, too? What are you going to do about it?"

"Daniel!" My mom came rushing over, trailed by Kate, Eric, and Dr. Chisolm. "What, for God's sake, was your father doing on the roof?"

"Just getting a breath of air," I lied badly. "He had a touch of claustrophobia."

"Morris never had claustrophobia in his life," she said. "Tell me the truth."

I met her eyes. "He's got to do this, Mom."

"That's the truth?"

I nodded. "And he said to tell you he loves you."

She looked back at me, took a quick breath, and grabbed on to the back of a chair for momentary support. "Can't you explain to me why he's putting himself through this?" she asked softly. "If I understood the reason, then it might be easier."

"It goes way back to when he was a teenager, before he met you," I told her. "If you want to know more than that, you've got to ask him."

She looked for a second like she was contemplating taking the elevator up to the penthouse and asking him right there, and trying to put a stop to this herself. Then she glanced at my father's face on the monitor. He was watching Liszt, waiting for the big man to move. Dad looked tense and haggard, but an almost imperceptible smile never left his lips. It transformed him, giving him an air of confidence and calmness beyond his exhaustion, as if he were somehow enjoying the pain of this struggle. Mom shrugged her shoulders. "Okay, Morris," she whispered. "If this is what you have to do, then win it."

Liszt reached a hand down to the chessboard and decisively took the knight, accepting Dad's sacrifice.

My father looked back at his old rival for a half second, and the bemused smile on his face became a tiny bit more pronounced. Without studying the board any further, my dad quickly made a bold pawn move.

"That's a very aggressive pawn thrust for black," the master said. "It's difficult to calculate it out fifteen or twenty moves in advance, but it doesn't look sound to me. The time pressure must be getting to Pratzer."

"No, is the best move," a heavily accented voice contradicted him. A man in an ill-fitting suit clambered up onto the podium next to the master. I recognized Former World Champion Contender Arkady Shuvalovitch. "Is exactly the right line for black," he said. "Only chance."

"But he only has three minutes left," the master said.

"Better than two minutes," Shuvalovitch observed, his eyes never straying from the position.

I realized that this graceless little man with a superb chess brain—who had once played for the championship of the world—could see something in the position that was beyond the ken of the master.

Liszt's own face tightened at my father's bold pawn advance, and he fired right back with a move of his own.

"They're into it now," the master said. "Black has no time to hesitate, and white is doing a superb job of moving quickly, too, not letting black think on his time."

They moved faster and faster, stroke and counterstroke, both of them hunched over the chessboard, slamming down pieces and hitting the clock so that their arms and hands were almost a blur. There must have been three hundred people in the common area now, reacting to every move with groans or applause. My dad was the crowd favorite—he had less than a minute left and everyone loves an underdog.

The funny thing was that my father didn't look scared now. He was a short, bald man, drenched in sweat and visibly trembling, but he somehow looked completely in control and even, momentarily, heroic—as if he had been born for this moment, and waited years for it, and now that it had finally arrived, he was ready and locked in. Time after time I thought he was lost, but he made bold move followed by bold move with an uncanny certainty, as if he were following a script he had already written out in his head.

My mother stood next to me and watched him play with shining eyes. She didn't know chess, but it didn't matter. As the crowd lustily cheered him on, she turned to me and whispered, "He's good, isn't he?"

"No, Mom," I told her, "he's great."

Liszt looked more and more worried. He was biting his knuckles and throwing constant glances over at my dad's clock, which showed less than twenty seconds. My father's king had joined his two pawns on their march across the board, and it was clear that Liszt could not stop them. So he sacrificed his rook for both black pawns, and now he was way down in material and clearly had a lost game, but my dad had only seventeen seconds left. If Dad's clock ran out before he checkmated Liszt, he would lose on time.

My father slid all the way forward on his seat, almost embracing the chessboard, taking less than a second per move. He was marching another pawn the length of the board to queen it. The crowd cheered his every step, as Liszt parried and retreated and tried his best to halt the pawn. Ten seconds left. Eight. Seven. I began to suspect that even if Dad queened the pawn he would never have time to win the game. Liszt must have reached the same conclusion—he looked more confident. Dad would never make it. Six seconds left. Five.

Dad's pawn was now one square away from queening, but he only had four seconds left. Three.

Dad moved his king and the crowd let out a collective sigh. It sounded like the air escaping from a punctured blimp as it sputters to the ground for a spectacular crash. Dad had blundered horribly. He had moved his king away from his pawn, allowing Liszt to take it with his own king. Liszt hesitated for a second, as if not able to believe his good fortune. Then he took Dad's pawn with his king, slammed his fist down triumphantly on the clock, and said: "It's over, Morris. Your last hope is gone. You lose."

Dad reached down and moved his knight in a black blur,

and said "Checkmate," and stopped his clock with one second left.

It slowly dawned on me that by grabbing the pawn with his king, Liszt had opened himself up to a hidden checkmate by Dad's knight and two bishops, and somehow in the whirl of time pressure my father had seen it.

Liszt looked down at the board and then reeled back as if he had been shot by a bazooka shell. "No," he muttered.

My father held out his hand. "Nice game."

Then the giant grandmaster was on his feet, shouting: *"This will not stand!* I already won. You left the playing area. I will appeal this. I won first prize!" He pushed over the chess table, and my dad jumped out of the way in the nick of time. Then Liszt grabbed a chair and brandished it like a weapon, and there was shouting and confusion, and the live feed from the camera cut out.

My mom grabbed my arm, panicked, and asked, "What's happening?"

"Liszt can't handle losing," I told her.

"Yes, but what happened to Morris?"

"I'm not sure," I admitted, worried.

"He'll be okay," Liu assured her.

"Yes, there are plenty of people up there to deal with this," Dr. Chisolm agreed, sounding a bit worried himself and punching buttons on his cell phone. "I'm sure everything's under control."

There was an eerie, charged silence in the common area as

three hundred people stared up at the two dark monitors. No one left. The throng of chess players milled around, waiting and whispering about the gargantuan struggle they had just witnessed. And then there was a *ping* and the doors to the private penthouse elevator opened. My father stepped out alone.

He looked very small and frail standing there, and even a little lost. He stumbled out of the elevator and blinked, as people called out questions to him about George Liszt and what had happened up in the penthouse. "He hit the referee with a chair," my father said, glancing around at the swirl of faces and the bright lights. "He's upstairs now. Talking to the hotel security." Then my dad spotted us and waved, and started to cross the carpet.

I took my mother's arm and led her toward him, but we had to fight our way through the crowd. Kate reached Dad first, and he put his hand on her shoulder as if for support. Then he saw us getting close and opened his arms, and the next thing I knew we had all joined him in a big family hug.

The crowd broke into applause—a loud and spontaneous ovation that kept getting louder second by second, but my father didn't seem to hear it.

I think his legs had pretty much given out because it felt like I was propping him up. The ovation from the crowd washed over us in waves as we stood there embracing, and then Dad looked at my mother and kissed her on the lips, and whispered to her and to all of us, "Let's go home."

CODA

Chess club was done for the day and so was I. It was a warm May afternoon and I had played four games and won two of them, which was a disappointing result for me these days. In the two months since the tournament I had climbed several hundred rating points to become a class B player and it was pretty clear that next fall I would make the travel team of the Looney Knights—the only sophomore on the squad. I realize that's not quite the same as cracking into the starting lineup of the New York Yankees, but progress is progress.

I wasn't studying chess that much, but three nights a week I was playing a game against my dad. He would set up two boards on our dining room table after dinner and I would sit down at one of them and Kate would reluctantly sit down at the other, muttering something like "According to the parenting books, too much chess at an early age can stunt a child's delightfully unformed mind . . ."

"Whereas unlimited talking on a cell phone can promote creativity and intellectual development?" Dad asked her. "Don't even go there. Today I want you both to play the black side of the French, try to trade off your weak bishops, and put as much pressure as you can on my center."

The funny thing was that for all Kate's complaining, she was developing into a ferocious player and was getting closer and closer to beating me. "Watch out," Dad warned. "The second sibling usually ends up kicking the butt of the first."

"Not in this family," I told him. "My butt remains unkickable."

He shot me his all-knowing grandmaster grin, which now flashed playfully in our dining room with some regularity, and whispered: "Sorry, Daniel. It's only a matter of time. She's got your number."

Don't get me wrong—Morris Pratzer had not undergone a dramatic transformation since winning the New York tournament. His pants were still too short, his scalp had grown balder, and his potbelly bigger, and during tax season he worked long hours at his accounting firm and came home so weary and detached that some nights he barely said five words to us.

But three times a week when we had family chess hour he seemed to come alive. We sat down together, with Mom hovering in the background brewing hot cider and doling out cookies.

Dad didn't want to play in any more tournaments, and I didn't push him. But he had rediscovered his love for the game, and he even visited my chess club once to talk about strategy in middle games. We had never had a grandmaster come before, and the club members were very excited. I was a little nervous, but he didn't try to wiggle his ears or arch his eyebrows. Instead, he stuck to his subject and even showed us some examples from his own old tournament games. Later, he played a simultaneous exhibition against our thirty-four club members and two faculty advisers and whipped us one and all, and my stock among the chess club nerds at having a cool dad rose to new heights.

Eric Chisolm had gotten into Harvard and was now the sole captain of the Looney Knights. Brad Kinney had been wait-listed at Princeton and had dropped off our chess team to concentrate on his grades and some upcoming national swimming events. He had also started volunteering at a senior citizens center. The rumor at school was that his father had threatened to kick him out if he didn't shape up. I passed Brad in the halls sometimes, and he nodded but never smiled or said anything friendly. He looked self-contained and angry, and I'm not sure his volunteer work was teaching him anything except to hide his nastiness and bide his time.

Okay, I'll be honest—that warm May afternoon when I lost two of four games in chess club, I blundered the last one away on purpose. My opponent seemed to be taking an eternity for each move, and I needed to get out of there fast. "Oh my God, I just dropped my knight. You win," I said, knocked over my king, and ran for the door.

I usually do my homework on the trip home, but a light rain had started falling, pattering on the metal ceiling of the school bus, and I couldn't concentrate. I gave up, stowed my books in my knapsack, and watched the houses get smaller and the yards shrink as we left the estate section behind and neared my own part of town.

I didn't go straight home, but rather I hurried to the main intersection of Broad and Elm, where the Public Transit bus from Manhattan stops on its meandering route through Essex County. The rain had slackened to a light drizzle, and I sat on the bench and waited, enjoying the balmy evening as the darkness took hold and the streetlights clicked on. I couldn't stop glancing at my watch and counting down the minutes.

Far down Broad Avenue, a large glowworm finally appeared in the distance. Car headlights darted around the bus as it crawled toward me. I stood up from the bench and watched it chug to a stop, and then the doors opened.

An old woman climbed carefully down the steps, and Liu was right behind her in tight jeans and a black leather jacket. She saw me waiting and smiled. "Jesus, Jersey boy, you do live out in the boonies."

I had gotten together with her half a dozen times since the tournament, but always in Manhattan. Now she was on my turf.

I helped her down the final step and took her shyly in my arms. Each time I saw Liu I felt a little awkward about touching her—half expecting her to pull away—but she never did.

I was starting to accept that I had my first girlfriend, and that she actually really liked me. "Thanks for coming," I told her.

She leaned into my hug and kissed me softly on the lips. "How long have you been waiting here, you bozo?"

"Just a minute or two."

"Liar," she said. "You're soaked. Okay, you wanted me, you got me. Show me the sights."

As we walked to my house, I pointed out the pathetic places of interest in my boring town—the elementary school where my mom teaches, the church that had been struck by lightning, the park where a few diehards were playing basketball under the lights, and the house where a murder had occurred seven years ago.

"Fascinating," Liu observed with her usual sarcasm. "No wonder out of all the places on earth your parents chose this town."

We reached my house and I was aware of how small and shabby it looked, even compared to some of the other homes on our block, but Liu didn't seem to care at all. "A house is a house," she said, "and this one seems nice enough." She marched right in and was soon giving my mom a hug and waving to my sister, who appeared for half a second and returned Liu's wave before disappearing back into her room.

"So, this is what he got for all his trouble," Liu said, walking over to our mantel and inspecting the large trophy that gleamed above the fireplace. It was inscribed with the date and name of the tournament and the words: GRANDMASTER

MORRIS PRATZER—FIRST PLACE, and there was a silver figure of a chess player raising both hands in triumph, a bishop clenched in one fist and a knight in the other. "I'm surprised he keeps it out here in public."

"Actually, I wanted to stow it in the garage, but they insisted," Dad told her, walking in from the back wearing an apron and wielding a spatula. He had come home early to barbecue burgers on the deck—a very rare event for a weekday. "How do you like your burger?" he asked Liu. "And how's your mom?"

"Rare and great," Liu told him, giving him a fond hug. "She's taken up the tango and having a ball with it. She sends you her best."

"Tell her hello back and that I'm still recovering from her karaoke party," Dad said with a grin, and headed back outside to check his barbecue.

We gobbled down all of Dad's burgers in record time, with french fries and salad. Mom had baked an apple pie and served it with vanilla ice cream. She kept smiling at Liu, and I could tell how much she liked her. "So how is your band going?" my mom asked Liu as we dug into the dessert.

"Great," Liu said. "We're playing a summer concert in Riverside Park in June. It's gonna be a battle of the bands—there will be three other bands playing and food and dancing on the grass. I'm hoping Daniel can come." She glanced at Kate. "Maybe you'd like to come, too?"

Kate looked torn for a long second. She normally makes

fun of everything I do and wouldn't be caught dead hanging out with me or any of my friends. But I could tell that a trip to a Manhattan concert tempted her. "I guess I'll tag along," she finally muttered.

After dinner Liu and I headed to the town rec center. "So how's Britney?" she asked me as we trudged through the dark streets, still damp from the rain.

"Good," I told her. "She's got a new boyfriend. A junior. Willie Magee. Model handsome. Captain of the wrestling team. He's also a real good guy."

"That didn't take her long," Liu noted.

"You had to figure it wouldn't," I said.

We heard the pounding music then, two blocks away, and saw the lights. "Wow," Liu said. "This is happening."

"Trust me," I told her. "I'll take you to all the best spots."

We walked inside the old wooden recreation center and rented skates, and I could tell right away that I had finally found something Liu wasn't good at. She kept her hands out for balance and penguin-walked over to the side wall. The music boomed and the whirling colored lights strobed her face and made her look disoriented and even a little scared. "First time on skates?" I asked.

"I'll get the hang of it and toast you in no time," she promised.

"I'm sure you will," I said. Then I skated away from her and did a fast lap, zigzagging as I approached her and stopping on a dime. "Two years of rec hockey," I said.

She stuck out her tongue at me. "Show-off. In New York we have better ways of spending our time. But this can't be so hard." She pushed off the wall and went for it, and fell right on her butt.

I skated over and held out my hands. "Nice technique."

"Laugh at me and you're dead meat," she warned, taking my hands. But she pulled a little too hard, and I ended up losing my balance and toppling over next to her.

"Hey," I said, "that's not even legal in hockey."

"Serves you right," she said. "Let's stay down here a minute, Dan."

So I sat down on the polished wooden floor next to her and put my arms around her a little protectively as skaters circled past us. Some of them were kids I had gone to elementary and middle school with. A few of them waved as they whirled by. Then there were older couples, and tots wearing bike helmets. Liu watched them also, and then looked into my eyes and whispered: "Hey, Patzer-face, where the hell have you brought me?"

"Skating night is the big event here," I told her. "And I'm a class B player now, soon to be a starting travel team member of the Looney Knights."

"Is that supposed to impress me?"

I held her a little tighter. "Also, I did something my father the grandmaster never did—I met a nice girl at a chess tournament."

"You get no credit for that. I picked you out," Liu told me.

"You did? But you were so rude to me . . ."

"I didn't like you at first," she admitted.

"What made you change your mind?" I wanted to know. "It wasn't my chess playing . . . ?"

"No," she said. "At first you seemed like just a nice dork, but then I saw you had some unexpected levels."

"Like a basement and an attic?" I probed.

She laughed. "I liked your relationship with your father," she told me. "It was complicated but sweet. Now be quiet. This is one of my favorites." A slow love song had come on, and she half closed her eyes and started to sing along to the words.

I held her in my arms, and for the first time I didn't feel shy or expect her to pull away.